After helping to capture a gang of
cow thieves, Deputy Sheriffs Alice
Fayde and Bradford Counter were
sent to investigate a murder. The
killer thought that he had been real
smart, battering his victim's face
beyond recognition and dumping the
body in the woods. Even if her body
should be found, the killer believed
it could not be identified and traced
back to him.
That was where he made his worst
mistake. He underestimated the
capabilities of the Rockabye County
Sheriff's Office laboratory technicians
– and the dogged persistence of the
deputies on his trail.

THE DEPUTIES

by

J. T. EDSON

This first hardcover edition published in Great Britain 1988 by
SEVERN HOUSE PUBLISHERS LTD of
40–42 William IV Street, London WC2N 4DF
by arrangement with Transworld Publishers Ltd., London.

British Library Cataloguing in Publication Data
Edson, J. T.
The deputies.—(Rockabye County series).
I. Title   II. Series
823′.914[F]   PR6055.D8
ISBN 0–7278–1594–6

Printed and bound in Great Britain

For Fred Wagstaffe and 'Banana' Bob
Reynolds although they insulted my
sylph-like figure and favourite split-cane
spinning rod.

CHAPTER ONE

WHEN a man steals another's stock in the Northern cattle-raising States, folks call him a rustler. Texans prefer to apply a blunter, more accurate term and say 'cow thief'.

Whatever name is used, the words conjure up a vision of dark nights on the open range; the smell of burning hair and hide as running irons alter brands, their users alert for the first warning sounds of an approaching posse.*

Altering conditions brought changes to ranching methods. No longer do almost numberless herds of half-wild longhorn cattle roam at will across the open range. Fences chop the land into easily-managed sections which aid the cowhand – his horse augmented by jeep and helicopter – in gathering and handling his charges.

The work of the cow thief has also been simplified by the new conditions.

The three cow thieves working in Rockabye County, Texas, on a moon-lit early October night needed neither horses, jeep nor helicopter. Instead they went on foot – tantamount to suicide when dealing with the fabled Texas longhorn but safe enough among the more placid, if better-beefed breeds of cattle which replaced it – to gather a dozen Hereford bullocks from a fenced-in pasture and, using electric-shock 'cattle prods', herded them up the ramp of the waiting truck.

With the loading completed, the thieves climbed into the cab of the truck and drove away from the scene of their crime. Their desination was not a ranch, whose owner would alter the brands and loose the cattle amongst his stock, but a slaughterhouse where the animals would be disposed of and all evidence of ownership destroyed; a far safer method for the men involved in the stealing.

* For a description of the old West's methods, read *The Cow Thieves*.

While methods of stealing and disposal might have changed, one thing remained constant. Cattle stealing always was and still remained a serious crime, to be prevented, if possible, by the local law enforcement officers.

Seated behind the truck's steering wheel, Red Wethley doubted if the local law would be around to interfere. By the time the rancher discovered his loss, returned to his home and telephoned a complaint to the nearest sheriff's sub-office, Red hoped to be out of the county at least and possibly already at the slaughterhouse. Once the cattle were unloaded and the truck washed down there was nothing to prove it other than what the signs on its sides announced, a removal truck belonging to an Inter-State company.

They were, Red conceded, still not out of danger, being on a narrow track leading to the distant ranch house. However ahead lay the second-class road which connected with Main Highway 90. Once on it, the removal truck would attract little attention. Red hoped that nobody would see them leaving the track. Witnesses had an unpleasant habit of remembering inconvenient details which the law followed up with dogged persistence.

At first it seemed that Red's desire to be unobserved would be respected. Then an elegant two-tone Rambler estate wagon swung into sight around a bend in the road. Red cursed under his breath, then relaxed as he watched the way in which the Rambler was weaving back and forwards across the road. A driver in such a condition was unlikely to remember seeing anything, except maybe a few pink elephants. So Red slowed down, meaning to let the Rambler pass the intersection before driving out. Unfortunately the estate wagon did not go by. Already travelling slowly, it swung and came to a halt blocking the mouth of the track.

'Damned drunk!' Red spat out, stopping the truck. 'Looks like he's passed out.'

'Looks that way,' agreed his brother Tom, sitting at his left side, and reached towards the horn button on the steering wheel. 'I'll soon wa—'

'Don't be *loco*!' Red snapped, slapping the hand away. 'We don't want noise. Get down and go tell him to move it.'

'Sure, big brother,' Tom answered and looked at the

8

third member of the party. 'You heard the man, Mig. Let's go do just that.'

Following Miguel Ortiz from the cab, Tom hesitated before going to carry out his brother's orders. Then he reached behind the passenger seat and pulled out a tyre-lever.

'What's that for?' Red demanded.

'Feller might not want to move,' Tom pointed out.

Looking at the vehicle blocking their escape, Red conceded that his younger brother had a point. Although leaning back and apparently too far gone in drink to make trouble, its driver appeared to be big enough to raise one helluva fuss happen he objected at being shaken awake and told to move on. Tom and Mig were both tall, lean, and well-schooled in the arts of all-in street fighting but precautions cost nothing. Every minute of delay added to the danger of the theft being discovered and the local law starting its hunt for the cow thieves. So Red raised no objecion to his brother taking the tyre-lever.

As he walked with Ortiz towards the Rambler, Tom formed conclusions similar to those of his brother. The moonlight allowed him to see something of the estate wagon's interior; enough for him to estimate the size of the driver and to take comfort from the feel of the tyre-lever in his hand.

The moon's glow illuminated the man at the Rambler's wheel, setting off his curly golden blond hair and an almost classically handsome face. Not that Tom paid much attention to the blond's features, being more concerned with his muscular development. Clad in a dark blue blazer, the driver's bulky torso and great spread of shoulders did not come as a result of a tailor's judicious padding. The right hand looked big and powerful as it rested on the steering wheel. His left arm lay along the top of the seat behind the vehicle's other occupant. Despite the excellent cut of the blazer, open-necked white sharkskin shirt and yellow silk cravat, the big blond conveyed an air of size, hard physical condition and great strength.

Despite that, he did not unduly worry Tom for he appeared to have passed out and gave no hint of knowing the two young men were approaching the Rambler. Nor did the passenger seem aware of the danger. Shadows prevented Tom from seeing more than that it was a woman who had also passed out. So she did not enter into his calculations at that moment. The man would be the danger.

'It must've been some party,' Ortiz remarked, halting by the Rambler's right front fender. 'They're both stoned.'

'He'll have a head on his head's head time I've done with him,' Tom answered and operated the door's handle with his left hand, the right holding the tyre-lever ready to strike.

On pulling open the door, Tom became aware that something was wrong. It might have been the way the big blond sat, with his left leg bent and resting on the seat under the right's thigh. Or it could have been an awareness that something was missing. Carrying two occupants that drunk, the interior of the car ought to have smelled like a moonshiner's still – but it did not.

Never given to quick, analytical thinking, Tom noticed the position of the blond's left leg and the absence of any whiskey smell but drew no conclusions from them. Instead he went ahead with his preconceived line of action. Moving closer, he reached towards the blond with the intention of hauling him from the driver's seat and ending any chance of opposition before it started.

Suddenly, before Tom's hand reached him, the big man moved. Thrusting down on and using his right foot as a pivot, the blond rose and turned his back on Tom. With his left arm and right hand supporting his weight, he leaned in front of his companion and shot his left leg to the rear. Driving back, the crêpe-soled shoe rammed into Tom's midsection with some force. For all that, Tom might have counted himself lucky. The big blond's kick landed higher than he intended. If the foot had struck the groin, at which it had been directed, pain would have incapacitated him. Instead it arrived hard enough to hurt and thrust him away from the car, but did not cause him to drop the tyre-lever.

After shoving Tom away, the blond heaved himself backwards out of the Rambler. The force of his jump carried him clear of the car as Mig slammed its door in an attempt to trap him or knock him off balance. Avoiding the door, the blond landed with his back to Tom. Carried by his momentum, he continued moving in Tom's direction and straightened up. In doing so, the blond confirmed the young cow thief's impression of his size. Standing a good six foot three inches in height, his great spread of shoulders trimmed down to a slim waist and long, powerful legs.

Realizing that the blond would be no easy match in a hand-to-hand brawl, Tom swung up the tyre-lever and lunged forward. At the same time Mig fanned his right hand into his jeans' pocket and slid a switch-blade knife from it. If he tangled with a feller that big, he intended to use something more effective than his bare hands. Pressing the stud, he flicked open the razor-sharp blade of the knife and prepared to launch an attack at the blond's back.

For his size, the man from the Rambler could move with considerable speed. Coming to a halt, he pivoted around to face Tom and brought up both arms. He held them, right wrist across the left, in the path of the descending arm as it drove the tyre-lever at him. Passing between the blond's hands, Tom's arm struck the bottom of the 'V' formed by his wrists and halted as if it ran up against a wall.

Before Tom could decide how he might counter the X-block, the blond's right hand slipped forward to grasp his wrist. Fingers like steel clamps crushed at the trapped limb with numbing power. Tom let out a croak of agony, opened his hand involuntarily and dropped the tyre-lever. At the same moment the blond turned, swinging Tom as if he weighed no more than a small child. Heaving Tom around, the blond flung him towards the advancing Mig Ortiz. Good luck alone saved Tom from being impaled on his companion's knife. Driving forward, the blade spiked through the side of Tom's windcheater. Then he collided with its wielder, arriving hard enough to tumble them both against the side of the Rambler.

From its idling purr, the truck's engine growled into active life. The blond either failed to recognize the danger implied by the sound, or ignored it. Springing towards the two young men as they tried to untangle themselves from each other, he shot out his hands. Tom and Ortiz each felt a set of powerful fingers take hold of the back of his neck. Even if they guessed what their captor planned, they were given no time to avoid it. Drawing the cow thieves' heads apart, the blond propelled them together again. Two skulls met with a solid 'thwack!' and he felt his burdens go limp in his hands. Even as he thrust Tom and Ortiz aside to collapse by the rear end of the Rambler, the blond heard his companion make her presence felt.

At first Red had watched the happenings by the Rambler with more annoyance than concern. Knowing his brother's and Ortiz's ability in a rough-house brawl, he expected that they would easily deal with the estate wagon's driver. Then Red realized that the big blond was acting in a peculiarly effective manner for a man fresh woken from a drunken stupor. In fact he moved like he was cold sober, had expected trouble and been ready to meet it. That implied the big blond was a peace officer of some kind. There could be no other explanation for the way he had used the Rambler to block the exit from the track.

Seeing Tom's second attack halted, Red knew he must do something. He had a revolver thrust into his belt, but did not draw it. Before he cut in to help his brother and Ortiz, he wanted to be sure that they had a clear avenue of escape. With that in mind he pressed his foot down on the accelerator. He planned to ram the rear end of the estate wagon, relying on the truck being powerful enough to push it aside without sustaining any damage. From all appearances, the big blond was still occupied in dealing with Tom and Ortiz. Red hoped that they would hold the blond's attention long enough for his purpose.

At which point Red became aware of the Rambler's second occupant. It seemed that she too had only been faking. Certainly she showed no sign of drunkenness as she swung out of the right front door. Closing it, she advanced with the intention of going around the front of the vehicle to help her companion.

Red hair, done in a flip style that was neat without being fussy, framed a most attractive face. Maybe the features were not classically beautiful, but they had warmth, charm, personality and strength of character. She stood maybe five foot seven in height, with a rich, shapely body that an open lightweight stadium coat did little to conceal. Under the coat, a plain blue blouse and black stretch pants set off her rich feminine curves without blatantly advertising them.

Hearing the increased volume of the truck's engine, the girl looked at it and came to a halt. Her next actions gave Red the final proof that he was tangling with peace officers rather than chance-met citizens. Turning to face the truck, she brought her right hand into view for the first time. It held an automatic pistol which Red assumed, by its size, shape and her sex, to be a .38 Colt Commander. With swift, trained precision she rested her forearms on the Rambler's bonnet, left hand gripping and supporting the right. Taking aim as the truck lurched into motion, she squeezed the automatic's trigger.

Red heard the crack of the shot mingled with a pop and hissing sound. Then the truck tilted and slewed violently as its left front tyre punctured. Cursing savagely, he fought to regain control and keep his vehicle moving in the Rambler's direction. He saw the girl change her point of aim, still lining the automatic downwards. Flame spurted across the Rambler again. Lead ripped into the right front tyre, collapsing it and bringing the truck to a jolting stop.

Snatching the revolver from his belt, Red gripped the door handle. Before he could open the door, he saw the girl raise her weapon to point in his direction.

After tossing the unconscious Tom and Ortiz aside, the blond jerked open the Rambler's left rear door. Leaning inside, he reached under a blanket on the back seat and drew out a Winchester Model '12 riot gun. Stepping back, he turned and ran towards the truck.

Quickly Red assessed the situation. Matched against the girl's automatic only, he might have taken a chance; but not when faced with the handgun and a weapon designed primarily to fire buckshot. At that range, in the big blond's obviously capable hands, the riot gun's load, nine .32 calibre balls, would be unlikely to miss. Nor would the cab of the truck offer Red protection against them.

'Don't shoot!' Red yelled, tossing the revolver from the window. 'I'm coming out.'

Standing well clear of the cab, the big blond held the riot gun waist high but trained on Red. The cow thief dropped to the ground, making sure that he kept his empty hands in plain sight.

'Lean against the cab,' the blond ordered in a cultured Texas drawl. 'Assume the posture.'

Placing the flat of his hands on the side of the cab, Red leaned forward at an angle which prevented him from making sudden moves. Without taking the riot gun out of line on Red, the blond moved backwards until he could see the rear of the truck.

'Need any help, Brad?' called the girl.

'If there's more of them, they're fastened in,' the blond answered. 'See to those two before they come round.'

Red turned his head and watched the girl walk around the Rambler. Slipping the automatic into the right pocket of her stadium coat, she took a set of handcuffs from the left. Already Tom and Ortiz were groaning their way back to consciousness, but she did not hesitate. Going to them, she bent over and deftly coupled the unresisting Tom's right wrist to Ortiz's left arm.

'Bring him over here, Brad,' she said, stepping away from the two young men.

'You heard the boss-lady,' the blond told Red. 'Let's go.'

At the Rambler, the girl covered Red while her companion placed the riot gun inside then handcuffed him. With their prisoners secured, the man and girl still did not relax. While the blond kept watch on the trio, she took a General Electric 'Voice Commander' hand-held radio from the rear of the wagon.

'Deputy Fayde to Sheriff Tragg,' she said into the microphone, her southern drawl attractive to the ears. 'Have picked up consignment at Staydon's ranch. Over.'

'How'd you get on to us?' Red asked sullenly.

The big blond smiled at the girl and replied, 'Just fortunate, I reckon.'

CHAPTER TWO

If Red had heard the conversation in the sheriff of Rockabye County's office about ninety minutes after his arrest, he would have discovered that more than blind chance had caused the deputies arrival at such an inopportune moment.

In the days of the old west, a sheriff worked out of a small plank or adobe building in the county seat's main street. Sheriff Jack Tragg operated from the third floor of the six-storey Department of Public Safety Building, which also housed the Headquarters Division of the Gusher City Police Department. In a room which looked more suitable to a business executive than a Texas lawman, he sat at his desk and listened to Woman Deputy Alice Fayde tell of the cow thieves' capture. Her partner was attending to the formalities of jailing the trio in the cell block on the fifth floor.

Tall, lean and tanned, Jack Tragg managed to convey the impression of being a typical old west sheriff despite wearing a lounge suit. He might have been clad in range clothes, fresh from riding with a posse, as he leaned back in his chair and propped a long right leg on the polished top of the desk.

'When we saw the truck, we figured it best not to just roll up and ask them to stop,' Alice said. 'Brad drove down the road like he was drunk and stopped so we blocked the track. Then we sat back as if we'd both passed out and they fell for it.'

'You did right,' Jack complimented. 'They'd've rammed you or started throwing lead if you'd played it any other way.'

Cow thieves no longer face the hangman's rope on capture. However, under Article 1441 of the Texas Penal Code, the theft of cattle carried a penalty of from two to ten years imprisonment. So the three men would have been unlikely to surrender without a fight. While he knew his two deputies' skill in the use of firearms, Jack was pleased that they had avoided a gun battle.

'How did you get on to them?' Alice inquired.

'Seems like young Wethley threw over a girl-friend after he made her pregnant,' the sheriff replied. 'Only he forgot how much she knew about him. She went to the local law and told them everything and they passed the word to me. Trouble was that she couldn't say where they planned to hit. So I had to send teams on rolling stake-out and hope one of you would connect.'

'It wor—' Alice began.

The centre of the three telephones on the desk buzzed, cutting off her words. Taking up the receiver, Jack listened to the voice at the other end. His eyes went to the girl's face and a slight frown creased his brow.

'Sure,' he said. 'I'll send a team out there now.'

'Oh no!' Alice groaned, realizing what the words meant, as the sheriff replaced the receiver.

'There's a reported "woman down" on the Morgan Turn-Off from Route 118,' Jack said. 'Will you and Brad take it?'

'Sure,' Alice agreed, knowing all the rest of the watch had gone home.

By virtue of its county-wide jurisdiction, the Sheriff's Office also acted as Gusher City's homicide bureau. Along with the specialist squads of the G.C.P.D., the deputies worked a two-watch rota; from eight in the morning to four in the afternoon and four up to midnight. If officers should be needed between midnight and eight o'clock, the permanently-manned Business Office called them from their homes.

So, while he said, 'will you', Jack had the right to assign the investigation to Alice and Brad. 'Woman down' meant that somebody had found a female body. All cases of unattended death were treated as homicide, so a deputy team would be required on the spot. Knowing this, Alice raised no arguments. Being on call twenty-four hours a day was the price one paid for belonging to the Sheriff's Office.

'I'll have a cameraman standing by downstairs,' Jack told

16

the girl. 'Take the Rambler. You'll find an r.p. out there. Call in if you need anything.'

'Yo!' Alice replied, standing up and taking her shoulder bag from the back of the chair.

Designed by Pete Ludwig with the specialized needs of policewomen in mind, the bag had a built-in holster, handcuffs pouch and ammunition case. It held in addition to the usual feminine items, her Colt Commander automatic – a .45, not the .38 Red thought a woman would carry – identification wallet, whistle, notepad and pens.

Leaving the sheriff, she walked along the passage by the watch commander's office and deputies' squadroom. One of the elevators' door slid open and she stepped inside before Deputy Sheriff Bradford Counter could emerge.

'What's up, boss lady?' he asked as she started the elevator going downwards.

'We've caught one,' she replied. 'Lordy lord, who'd be a peace officer?'

The answer was that both she and Brad would.

Alice Fayde had joined the Gusher City Police Department because she felt it offered the employment she was best suited to perform. After serving as a uniformed rookie in the Bureau of Women Officers, she had graduated to the Detective Bureau. There she worked out of such diverse divisions as Evans Park, in the slum area known as the Bad Bit, and snob Upton Heights. Then she spent time in specialist squads, Traffic, Juvenile and finally Narcotics. Finally she earned, on merit, a coveted appointment to the Sheriff's Office. Not as the usual run of woman deputy – handling female prisoners, attending to clerical duties or riding a telephone switchboard – but as an active member of the Office.

Crashing the barriers into the previously all-male Sheriff's Office had not been easy. At first the male deputies doubted if a woman would be of any use except as a decoy or to interview female suspects. However Alice and another appointee, Joan Hilton, ignored the men's opinions and near-hostility, working until they had finally proved themselves useful members of the department.

Unlike Alice and the other deputies, Brad had come straight to the Sheriff's Office without first serving in the

G.C.P.D. At first his appointment caused gloomy predictions of failure. Despite his passing as honour graduate at the University of Southern Texas' Police Science and Administration class and going through. the Federal Bureau of Investigation's exacting twelve-week police officer's training course with distinction, the other deputies felt that he lacked practical experience in law enforcement.

Brad proved the predictions false. Coached by veteran deputy, Tom Cord, he developed fast into a competent officer. When a load of buckshot cut Tom down, Brad had teamed with Alice to hunt the killer.* Since the successful end of their first case, Alice and Brad had welded into a smoothly-functioning team. Less than three weeks had elapsed since their efforts brought about the capture of a murderous gang hiding in Rockabye County before attempting to escape across the border into Mexico.†

Although born into one of Texas' wealthiest families, Brad showed a remarkable affinity for law enforcement work. Possibly it stemmed from being a descendant of Mark Counter, gun fighter, peace officer – and considerable of a hand with the ladies – back in the 1870s.‡ If so, Brad inherited his great-grandfather's dexterity with firearms. While he wisely produced a riot gun to deal with Red Wethley, Brad had a .45 Colt Government Model automatic under his left arm in a Hardy-Cooper spring-shoulder holster. He could handle it with the speed and efficiency of an old-time gun fighter. In addition, he equalled his forebear's legendary strength and skill in a rough-house.

It was a great comfort for Alice to know she was working with a partner who, as well as being a shrewd detective, could draw his gun in around half a second and hit what he aimed at on doing so. Also Brad possessed a thorough knowledge of judo, karate, boxing and plain, old-fashioned knock-down-and-drag-out brawling. Even in jet-age Texas such abilities had their uses.

While riding down in the elevator, Alice told Brad what was taking them out on an investigation instead of to their beds. A tall, grey-haired man was waiting for them on the

* Told in *The Professional Killers*.
† Told in *The ¼ Second Draw*.
‡ Mark Counter's story is told in the author's Floating Outfit books.

ground floor. Dressed in a leather windcheater, jeans and hunting boots, he carried a wooden case and a Polaroid camera swung from its strap on his right shoulder. He was Sam Hellman, a detective of the Scientific Investigation Bureau who specialized in photography.

'Hi Alice, Brad,' he greeted. 'What's it all about?'

'A "woman down" on Route 118,' Alice answered.

Hellman made a wry face. 'I always get the better ones. Do we use my heap or take yours?'

'We're going up in the Rambler,' Alice told him.

'Nice,' Hellman commented.

'Our car's with the mechanics,' Brad explained. 'I'd best get the murder kit from it, Alice.'

'We'd better take it along,' she replied. 'Let's get this show on the road.'

With that the girl led the way through a rear entrance and into the official parking lot. There, arranged in a geometric pattern for ease of departure, stood vehicles of many kinds. Crossing to where a pair of mechanics were working on a black and white Oldsmobile Super 88 deputy car, Brad unlocked the boot. From it he took a leather case which held equipment of use during the primary stages of a murder investigation.

Walking to the Rambler, Brad passed the case to Hellman in the rear seat and climbed into the front. While Brad reported their departure and destination to the dispatcher at Central Control, using the Voice Commander radio, Alice started the engine. Then she drove the Rambler by the checker's cabin at the gates and into the almost deserted streets of the town.

CHAPTER THREE

THE Morgan Turn-Off was two miles from Gusher City, one of several dirt roads which joined Route 118. Winding through rolling, wooded country, it eventually reached the village of Morgan's Corners. Driving towards the Turn-Off, Alice saw a black and white radio patrol car belonging to the G.C.P.D. and a hot-rod parked at the side of route 118. The r.p.'s interior lights were on and a uniformed policewoman sat inside comforting a pretty blonde girl. Leaning against the r.p.'s front door, a patrolman spoke into the transmission microphone of the car's radio. A second harness bull stood with a tall teenager by the hot-rod.

Swinging away from the teenager as the Rambler came to a halt, the second patrolman walked towards it. He looked tired and unready to suffer stray, joy-riding kibitzers gladly. Being used for undercover work, the Rambler carried nothing to show it belonged to the Department of Motor Vehicles. So he bore down on it grimly. It had been his team's day in court, which had prevented him from getting any sleep during his off watch hours. What he had just seen along the Turn-Off did nothing to make him feel amiable.

'All right, lady,' he said, trying, if not entirely succeeding, to sound polite. 'It's nothing. Pass on.'

'The name's Fayde,' Alice answered, holding out her id. wallet with its badge and identity card. 'Deputy sheriff.'

Instantly the patrolman lost his thinly-veiled belligerence. The change did not spring from knowing that a deputy sheriff held equivalent rank and disciplinary powers to a Patrol Bureau lieutenant. Before him sat another peace officer. One who had been on watch since four the previous afternoon and might spend the remaining hours of darkness working on the 'woman down' case.

'I'd heard Jack Tragg used da— women on investigation

teams, ma'am,' the patrolman said as he opened the driver's door. 'But I'm damned if I believed it.'

'You'll be taking the vote from us next,' Alice smiled and swung out of the Rambler. 'What's it all about?'

'We met these two kids coming into town fast. The boy stopped and told us they'd found a stiff while they were out doing the moon-and-June bit. So we called in and Cen-Con said for us to come take a look. The girl was near on hysterical, but Karney, our gal, got her quietened down.'

Glancing at the r.p., Alice nodded. She could rely on the policewoman to cope unaided with the girl.

'Is there a body?' Alice asked.

'Yeah,' the patrolman replied. 'I saw it from the road up there, didn't go right to it. The wind was blowing from it and I knew there was no need. My partner's just calling for the m.e. and meat wagon.'

By that time Brad and Hellman had come from the Rambler, each carrying his kit box. Turning towards them, Alice gave her orders. As senior deputy present, she had command of the investigation. Having won her promotion on merit, she felt no self-consciousness about telling the men what she wanted doing.

'Go with the patrolman and start taking your general shots, will you, Sam,' she said. 'Brad and I'll be along when we've talked to the boy.'

'Yo!' Hellman replied, giving the old-time cavalry response to an order.

While Hellman and the patrolman went off along the dirt road, Alice walked over to the hot-rod with Brad. Studying the boy by it, they liked what they saw. He wore a sports jacket, sweater and grey slacks. Handsome, clean, his face had an open friendliness somewhat marred by a worried and sick expression.

'Hey,' Alice greeted, taking a pen and notebook from her bag. 'Do you feel like talking?'

'Are you reporters?' the boy countered, a touch defensively.

'Nothing so glamorous,' Alice replied. 'We're deputy sheriffs.'

'No kidding?'

'I've got the badge to prove it,' Alice smiled. 'Woman Deputy Fayde, it says. And you are—?'

'Al— Allen Jeffords,' the youngster answered, eyeing Alice's figure with open admiration. 'My address is 14 Monstel Street. Look. How soon can I take Betty home? Her folks will flip, us being out at this hour.'

'We have to ask questions first,' Brad pointed out.

'When we're through, we'll have the policewoman go with you to explain to Betty's parents,' Alice promised. 'Why did you come out here?'

'We weren't doing anything wrong!' Allen bristled.

'I never said you were,' Alice replied.

'We'd been to a late movie, but it was crap. So we decided to come for a drive before we went home is all.'

'Do you come here often?' Brad asked.

'How do you mean, "here"?'

'To the Morgan Turn-Off.'

'Here or some other turn-off. They all look alike in the dark.'

'How'd you find the body?' Brad continued while Alice recorded the conversation in her notebook.

'We were necking, then started horsing around. Betty jumped out of the heap and ran along the side of the road. When I caught up to her, she swerved and started to go down the slope. She couldn't stop running when she saw the woman's legs sticking out from between two bushes.'

'What'd you do then?' Brad prompted gently.

'I – I got Betty back to the car. She was taking it bad, nearly hysterical. So I got her in the heap and headed for Gusher City as fast as I could. Maybe I should oughta gone back and seen if the wo – it – sh – the woman was still alive.'

'Was there any reason to think she might be?' Alice asked.

'N – I don't know. I didn't stop to look,' Allen croaked, his face working as if to hold down nausea. 'L – lord! The smell—'

'You did the right thing, *amigo*,' Brad assured him.

'I'll go along with that,' Alice agreed. 'Did you see any cars on or just leaving the Turn-Off, Allen?'

'No.'

'Thanks for your help,' Alice said, closing the notebook. 'I'll ask the girl a few questions before we go up, Brad.'

'Do you have to?' Allen put in. 'I mean like right now?'

'I'm afraid I do,' Alice stated.

'Dont you worry, *amigo*, Brad told the youngster. 'Alice'll do it real easy. Say, did you build the heap?'

Leaving Brad to distract and keep Allen occupied, Alice went to the r.p. car. It said much for her ability that she extracted the girl's story without undoing the policewoman's work. Betty confirmed Allen's story without being able to add to it. Nothing about the girl suggested to Alice's trained senses that she or the boy had guilty knowledge. However a peace officer rarely took anything at its face value.

'We'll not keep you much longer, Allen,' she promised, returning to the hot-rod. 'Let's go see how Sam's getting on, Brad.'

Alice directed the beam from a powerful electric torch, out of the murder kit, on to the ground as she and Brad walk along the Turn-Off.

'No chance of tyre-tracks on here,' she said.

'This short, springy grass won't hold footprints worth a damn either,' Brad replied.

That proved to be the case, for they reached where the patrolman stood at the side of the road without finding tyre marks or tracks. Halting at the man's side, Alice looked around her. They had come about two hundred yards but were hidden from Route 118 by trees and a curve in the road. A slope fell away from the road and Sam Hellman was working with his camera on the level ground at the bottom of it. Lining his camera at where a pair of bare legs showed between two dogwood bushes, he took another photograph. However he waited to check the result before turning in Alice and Brad's direction.

'I've got the general shots. Come down and take a look at her.'

Moving cautiously in Indian file, Brad and Alice went down the incline. The torch's light revealed no tracks, even the marks of Hellman's recent descent did not show in the short grass.

'Might in daylight,' Brad commented. 'But I doubt it.'

The body lay in deep shadows, on its back and between the two bushes. Only the legs emerged into the moonlight. They were shapely, with well-developed muscles, and clearly feminine.

Slowly Alice advanced the torch's light. A brief bikini

pantie in a leopard skin pattern came into view. Then the torso, its waist curving in and out with sensual grace to the tiny matching bra which inadequately covered the full mounds of the bust.

Sucking in her breath, Alice glanced at Brad. Every instinct she possessed warned her that they were in for something bad.

There were six bullet holes in the torso. One below and to the left of the navel, the second to the right and level with it. Two more had entered below her breasts. The fifth had punctured the left nipple and the last had made its hole in the centre of her chest just over the bra. Set off by the brief bikini, the body had magnificent curves.

And then Alice illuminated the face.

Only it no longer looked like a face. The features had been battered hideously. Blood, dried black and evil-looking, coated the ruin. The nose had no shape, only ruptured pulp, the teeth showed jagged and broken through the cut, swollen lips. Where the eyes had been were clots of blood. There was no hair, only a faint black ash, on the skull.

During her time as a peace officer Alice had seen many bodies. Yet she could not remember anything as horrid as the shape at her feet. If anything the gorgeous physique of the dead woman made the sight worse. Involuntarily Alice turned her head away. Nor was she alone in the reaction. Brad made a low, disgusted noise in his throat and looked up the slope. Letting out a growl of distaste, Hellman took a pace to the rear. He felt his heel sink into something soft and sticky.

'What's this?' he asked and Alice turned the light his way.

At first Hellman thought he had stepped into a pile of human faeces. However the gooey mass under the hard crust looked greyish, not brown.

'Somebody's fetched up their guts here,' Hellman commented.

'Not the kids, either,' Alice went on. 'It's been here some time. Photograph it, Sam. Then you'd best put it in a bag and let S.I.B. see it, Brad.'

'Sure,' Brad replied, setting down and opening the murder kit. he took out a plastic bag and wooden scoop. 'Do we search the bushes?'

24

'Best leave it until daylight,' Alice decided. 'S.I.B.'ll want to handle that end of it. They dearly love to get out in the fresh air— Only not at night.'

While the S.I.B. possessed the facilities and trained personnel to make the search, they could do nothing before morning. However Alice did not want to add to their work by having Brad and the patrolman moving among the bushes and possibly damaging evidence.

'Hey!' called a voice from the slope. 'When do I get around to seeing the body?'

A tall, slim young man in a short white jacket stood with the patrolman and two white uniformed attendants holding a stretcher hovered in the background.

'Come on down, doc,' Alice replied. 'Keep your men behind you and stay to the left of that rock half-way down.'

Working with unhurried precision, Hellman gathered his scene-of-the-crime photographs. Then he moved aside and allowed the medical examiner to approach the body. After making his examination, the m.e. turned to the deputies. He had cultivated an intense, studious air as a means of hiding the revulsion he felt at the sights his work brought him into contact with almost daily.

'The gun shot wounds caused death,' he said. 'The bullets are still inside. However she was battered on the face either while still alive or shortly after death.'

'Any idea when she died?' Alice asked.

'The *rigor mortis* has almost gone. From the greenish-blue coloration of the veins and abdomen, decomposition is setting in. There are some insect larvae in the mouth. Two to three days ago. I can't bring it closer than that without a more detailed examination.'

'That'd make it Monday or Tuesday,' Brad said. 'Was she killed here, doc?'

'I'd say "yes". Although I won't know for sure until I've checked the post-mortem lividity state of the body.'

'One thing's for sure,' Hellman commented. 'She didn't drive through the streets in that outfit.'

'Can I take a look at her, doc?' Alice inquired.

'I've done all I can,' the m.e. replied.

Taking a can of blue powder from the murder kit, Alice traced an outline of the body on the ground. After tossing the can to Brad, she took a deep breath and knelt down outside the powder line. Lifting the cold, clammy left hand, she looked at it.

'No wedding ring or other jewellery,' Alice said over her shoulder. 'Did you notice how short her nails are, doc?'

'No,' the m.e. admitted. 'I didn't look at them.'

'They are short,' Brad said, looking over Alice's head.

'My daughter's just started secretarial school,' Hellman put in. 'She's always bitching about having to keep her nails short while she's typing.'

'The B.W.O. rule we have to keep our nails short, too,' Alice answered. 'But not like this. They're cut down to the quick. Yet she cares for her hands.'

'Could be her line of work doesn't let her have long nails,' Brad suggested.

'That's my partner said that,' Alice announced in an admiring tone. 'Now all we have to do is wait and he'll tell us what kind of work.'

'I leave that to you, boss-lady,' Brad grinned. 'You're supposed to be the authority on women.'

'I'm not sure how that was meant,' Alice smiled back.

Only by such light banter could peace officers throw off their feelings in the face of death.

'Can I take the body now, Miss Fayde?' asked the m.e.

'Sure, doc. I'll take the bikini off for you and turn it over to the S.I.B., if you want me to.'

'Thank you,' the m.e. said and signalled his attendants forward.

Showing deft, almost casual ease the attendants lifted the body without disturbing the powder outline and placed it on the stretcher. Alice decided to leave the removal of the bikini until the body was in the ambulance, so stood aside and watched the men carry it up the slope. Then she turned to her companions.

'There's nothing more we can do here,' she said. 'Let's go back to town.'

'Do you want a stake-out here, Alice?' Brad asked.

'No. We'll have the local house send a r.p. out at sun-up and S.I.B.'ll be around early.'

'It'll not do the lab shiny-butts any harm to get up early,' Brad grinned.

'Yah!' Hellman sniffed, sensing an attack on his department. 'I've never seen anybody but janitors in the deputies' squadroom afore half past nine.'

'Somebody's got conscience troubles,' Alice whispered to Brad, making sure her words reached Hellman's ears. Then she put aside the levity and looked around. Brad had collected the vomit and it was now in the murder kit. She could see nothing to delay their departure. 'Let's go.'

On Route 118, Alice told the patrolmen to escort Tommy and Betty home. Then she crossed to and climbed inside the ambulance. Leaving the head covered, she drew aside the sheet from the body. Making a wry face, she set about removing the bikini. While drawing off the pantie, she noticed the absence of pubic hairs. Not that the discovery surprised her. Wearing such a scanty costume called for their removal. However the lack of hairs made the task of discovering the victim's identity more difficult.

Covering the now naked body, Alice backed out of the ambulance. Brad brought another plastic bag from the kit and held it open for her. Made up specially for the S.I.B., the bag had a draw-string with a cardboard tag attached. After examining the bikini for maker's labels, and finding none, Alice placed it into the bag. Closing the mouth of the bag and fastening the string, Alice took out her pen.

'*Jane Doe*,' she wrote on the tag. '*Morgan Turn-Off, approx. 200 yds. from Route 118. Deputies Fayde and Counter.*'

While Brad put the bag into the kit, Alice turned the Rambler. Hellman and Brad boarded the vehicle and she drove after the r.p., hot-rod and ambulance back to Gusher City.

The deputies found Jack Tragg waiting for them in the entrance hall of the Department of Public Safety Building. While Alice told the sheriff of their findings, Brad arranged with the desk sergeant to hand the bikini and bag of vomit to the S.I.B. when its members reported on watch.

'It's a bad one, sir,' Alice was saying as Brad joined her.

'I'll have a search team sent out there as soon as it's daylight,' Jack promised. 'Anything else?'

'It's not much of a chance, but could you ask Missing Persons if they have anybody to fit her general description,' Alice replied.

27

'Sure. I'll leave word for Ric Alvarez to ask as soon as they come on watch. You two had best log off now.'

'There's not much we can do before daylight,' Alice admitted. 'We'll come in around half past one, if that's all right with you, Brad.'

'Sure,' Brad agreed, although that meant they would be starting work before the official time. 'S.I.B. might have some lead to who she is by then.'

'Let's hope they have,' Alice breathed, thinking of the battered body. 'I want to get whoever killed her.'

CHAPTER FOUR

'THEN you've no idea of the woman's identity?'

The words came to Alice and Brad as they stepped out of the elevator at half past one in the afternoon. Alice now wore a bolero jacket, grey blouse and a denim skirt, while Brad had on a sports jacket, open necked shirt, silk cravat and flannels. Looking along the passage, they found First Deputy Ricardo Alvarez talking to a tall, slim young man they recognized.

'Not yet,' Ricardo answered with barely concealed irritation. 'The Public Relations Bureau has given all we have to your paper, Mr. Vassel.'

One of the *Gusher City Mirror*'s most intellectual reporters, Tony Vassel had a sallow, reasonably handsome face and short-cropped brown hair. He wore a grey suit, psychedelic shirt and no tie. All in all, he looked neater and more composed than when the deputies last saw him. That was understandable. The meeting had been during the Tom Cord case and Vassel was fleeing from a lady's bedroom under the impression that her husband had returned home unexpectedly.

'I just thought I'd come up and see if there were any new developments,' Vassel declared.

'There aren't,' Alvarez stated bluntly. Hey, Alice, Brad.'

Opening his mouth to protest at the curt dismissal, Vassel looked over his shoulder. Instantly his mouth snapped shut. His sallow cheeks reddened slightly and he turned to walk by the deputies into the elevator.

'That was Vassel of the *Mirror*,' Alvarez remarked as the elevator doors slid together hiding his unwelcome visitor.

'We've met,' Alice replied. 'The displeasure was mutual.' What did he want?'

'Came up to ask if we'd identified your victim yet. Too

important to wait for the regular P.R. hand-outs, I suppose. Now I reckon he'll be writing in tomorrow's *Mirror* how incompetent we are.'

'Or start his usual screams about banning the sale of firearms,' Brad growled. 'His kind always dig up that one when somebody gets shot.'

'Yeah—' Alvarez began, the light of battle glinting in his eyes.

'We've got work to do,' Alice interrrupted quickly. 'And we're going to start right *now*, before you pair get to damning the stupidity of anti-firearms legislation. Is there anything for us, Ric?'

A faint grin twisted the watch commander's lips. Five foot ten in height, handsome as a Hollywood latin matinee idol, Alvarez moved with the grace of a bullfighter. He wore a khaki uniform shirt and slacks, a .45 Colt Commander hanging in a combat bikini holster on the right side of his official waist belt.

Along with Brad, Alvarez – and many other peace officers – believed banning the sale and ownership of firearms to be stupid and impractical. All such laws did was disarm the law-abiding citizen. No criminal would be deterred from going armed by legislation making the possession of firearms illegal. However Alvarez took Alice's point, grinned and answered her question.

'There's a negative from Missing Persons. S.I.B.'s search report's come in, that's a negative. And F.I.L.'s sent in their preliminary. I wonder how Vassel got by Willy Jacobs?'

'There was a rookie harness bull on the desk when we came through,' Brad replied. 'Likely Vassel told him some tale and got passed through.'

'Willy'll have his hide if he did,' Alice smiled, knowing how Sergeant Jacobs ran the reception desk with a rod of iron. 'Let's make a start, Brad.'

The deputies worked out of a large, cool room that looked nothing like the old western sheriff's office. Two lines of four desks, each with a telephone and typewriter, stretched across the room. Filing cabinets lined one wall instead of a rack holding Winchester rifles and shotguns. The Office's assault armament – riot guns, M.1 carbines, Thompson sub-machine guns, telescope-sighted rifles and Federal gas gun kits – were kept in the two boxes which flanked the connecting door to the watch commander's office.

None of the day watch were in the office when Brad and Alice entered. Turning to the right, Brad looked at the bulletin board. Alice went to the desk at the left of the main doors and signed on in the log. Then, while Brad logged on, she removed the 'off watch' strips from their names on the roster board. From there, they went to their desk.

Taking their seats, they each took a report. Alice glanced at the Missing Persons Bureau's statement that no woman answering the victim's description had been reported missing. Brad found that the S.I.B.'s search team had been over the area thoroughly but found nothing, no tracks or evidence of any kind, to help the investigation. That left the Firearms Investigation Laboratory's findings.

'The bullets are .38 Smith & Wesson calibre, two hundred grains, metal-jacketed,' Alice told Brad as she read the report. 'Rifling is right hand twist, seven grooves. Three of them are good enough for comparison purposes.'

Then she paused, waiting to see if he could identify the make of gun. Brad had made an extensive study of hand guns and liked to match his knowledge against that of the F.I.L. crew. However, for once, he looked puzzled.

'.38 Smith & Wesson. A two hundred grain *jacketed* bullet?'

'That's what the man says.'

'And *seven* right-hand twist grooves in the rifling?' Brad continued. 'All right, I'll buy it. What kind of gun?'

'F.I.L. say one of those imported war-surplus British revolvers. A Webley, Albion or Enfield. They all fire the .38 Smith & Wesson and have the same style of rifling.'

An angry grunt broke from Brad. 'A three-eight, two hundred grain, jacketed bullet. What else could it be? The usual commercial load for the .38 Smith & Wesson is a one hundred and sixty grain lead bullet. The British had to jacket their load because a lead bullet's classed as a dum dum under the Geneva Convention.'

'So F.I.L. won one,' Alice smiled, then her face became sober as she picked up the next sheet of paper.

Looking over Alice's shoulder, Brad studied the two

sketches of a woman's bikini-clad torso. The F.I.L. experts had worked in conjuction with the medical examiner to supply what might prove to be relevant information. The first torso, a front view, had the bullet wounds' positions marked on it, numbered from one to six to indicate the possible order in which they had been fired. The second sketch, a side view, had gradually inclined lines showing the estimated angles of the bullets' flight. All but one had entered at a downwards slant. The odd bullet out, sixth to be fired, went into the left breast on a level flight.

'F.I.L. figure the killer was moving in on her,' Alice said, reading the message at the side of the sketches. 'On the fourth and fifth shots, below the navel and up here under the right breast, there are increasing traces of scorching. On the sixth shot there is actual burning which means the gun wasn't more than a couple of inches from her when it was fired.'

Brad studied the sketches for a few seconds without speaking, then he turned his attention to Alice.

'How tall was she?'

'About my size.'

'Then he couldn't have shot down at her to have the bullets enter at these angles with them both on level ground.'

'That's for sure,' Alice admitted, accepting the male gender her partner applied to the unknown killer. 'Unless he was using shoulder-high pointed fire.'

'Not even then,' Brad corrected. 'The last shot went in level.'

'What're you driving at, Brad?' Alice asked.

'I think the killer was standing on the slope and shooting down as she came up at him.'

'It doesn't seem possible,' Alice objected.

'Why not?' Brad countered. 'Women can stand up to more pain than any man. And the .38 Smith & Wesson doesn't have much shock or stopping power. I've a friend, a white hunter in Kenya, was issued with a Webley .38 by the Army in the Mau Mau Emergency. He wrote one time and told me that he'd hit a charging terrorist six times without stopping him, using it. One of his askaris had to wind up the deal with the butt of his rifle.'

'Nice friends you have,' Alice said, taking a file cover from the desk's drawer and putting the reports into it.

'What do you think of it as a theory?' Brad inquired.

'It's no better, nor worse, than F.I.L.'s. I'll mention it to Mac McCall when he comes on watch.'

'Don't tell him it's my idea – unless it comes out to be right.'

Giving her partner a look which bounced right off him, Alice returned the file to the drawer and stood up. 'Let's go see if the m.e. or S.I.B. can give us any more.'

The medical examiners' department shared the basement with the indoor pistol range; although separated from it by thick, soundproof walls. A short, tubby and – considering the work he performed – remarkably jovial featured man in a blood-smeared white smock came into the department's small reception room in answer to Brad's press on a bell button.

'Good afternoon,' the m.e. greeted. 'You caught the 'woman down' last night, huh?'

'Sure, doc,' Alice replied. 'Can you give us anything to go on?'

'Not much. She's aged between eighteen and twenty-five. I'd say around twenty-three. Natural blonde, we found enough hairs between the legs to tell that. The bullets killed her, although some of the blows to her face were struck just before she died.'

'Colour of eyes?' Alice asked tonelessly, writing down the information in her notebook and wishing the m.e. did not sound so damned matter-of-fact about the killing.

'I don't know.'

'How's that?' Brad inquired.

'Both eyes had been repeatedly struck until the balls were mashed out of shape,' the m.e. answered; and he no longer sounded matter-of-fact. 'The nose is damaged beyond re-building, the teeth so badly battered that I doubt if her dentist would know them.'

'Are we dealing with a sadist, doc?' Alice breathed.

'Possibly, Miss Fayde. Or it could have been done to prevent identification. I've had her fingerprinted. The facial wounds are peculiar. Some of them appear to have been caused by a hard, straight object.'

'By the barrel of a revolver?' Brad suggested.

'Hardly likely. The indentations were V-shaped. I never saw a revolver with a square barrel.'

'Not square,' Brad corrected. 'Six-sided. All those British service revolvers have hexagonal barrels. Externally, I mean.'

'One of them could have done it then,' the m.e. stated. 'But the other wounds were round in shape, as if they'd been made by a half-inch ball-bearing. From the number of them in the region, I'd say the rounded object was used to damage the eyes.'

'Those British revolvers all have a lanyard ring fitted to the butt,' Brad explained. 'The holder for the ring is a round ball about that size. F.I.L. might have a Webley in their collection—'

'I'll call them and ask,' the m.e. decided.

'Was there any sign of sexual assault?' Alice asked.

'None. She wasn't a virgin, but hadn't been touched before she was killed.'

'And there's nothing more you can tell us?'

'Only that she was in excellent physical condition. Her muscular development was remarkable.'

'Could be in show-biz, Alice,' Brad said. 'How about the time of death, Doc?'

'Monday night. I'd guess at after eight o'clock, but I can't get it any closer. She'd eaten a heavy meal during the evening. Trouble being the digestive juices continue to operate after death and there wasn't much left. I sent what there was to the lab.'

'Thanks, doc,' Alice said. 'I'm sorry we took up so much of your time.'

'That's all right,' the m.e. replied. 'I only wish I could give you more. I'll send up the full necropsy report as soon as I can.'

From the basement, Alice and Brad rode an elevator to the fourth floor. The S.I.B.'s various departments occupied the whole floor. Entering the reception area, the deputies told the policewoman on duty why they had come. Pressing one of the buttons on her telephone, she spoke to somebody.

'Lieutenant Cortez will see you in his office,' she said, hanging up the receiver and indicating the room in question.

If Ramon Cortez had been born in Hollywood, he might have made a good living playing villainous Mexican bandits in movies. Small, stocky, with a face that only a mother could love, he was one of the country's top police scientists.

'We've not much for you yet,' he told Alice and Brad when they entered. 'So far we've not broken down the contents of that vomit and there was nothing at the scene of the crime. That leaves the bikini.'

'Which, knowing our luck, could have been bought in half the five-and-dimes in Texas,' Brad commented wryly.

'Your luck's changed,' Cortez informed him. 'It's genuine leopard skin, not a nylon print imitation. Top quality workmanship, but no maker's name. You wouldn't get it from a five-and-dime.'

'That's for sure,' Alice agreed.

'We checked for hidden marks,' Cortez went on. 'It's new, never been cleaned. We came up blank.'

'Can I sign it out, Ray?' Alice inquired. 'If it was bought in town, there can't be many places it could come from.'

'Go to it,' Cortez replied. 'I'll let you know as soon as we've anything on the vomit.'

'Mind if I use the phone while you fetch the bikini?' Brad asked.

'Feel free,' Cortez answered, with the casually helpful air of one who would not be inconvenienced by agreeing.

'I'm calling the firearms Registry, Alice,' Brad said as the lieutenant left. 'It's a long shot, but I'm going to ask for a list of all registered Webley, Albion and Enfield .38s in the county.'

'It's worth trying,' Alice agreed. 'Let's hope the bikini gets us somewhere. We've nothing else to go on.'

CHAPTER FIVE

'Erotica Inc., yet!' Brad said as he drove Unit SO 12 towards Green Valley in search of a shop by that name. 'It's a new one on me.'

'And me,' Alice admitted. 'And I was born in Gusher City.'

The area into which they entered had become a gathering point for artists, college students and other assorted 'intellectuals'. It hardly seemed the part of town in which to search for the supplier of a genuine leopard-skin bikini. However the deputies had been given a lead and so followed it up, unlikely or not.

Although neither of the exclusive dress shops Alice and Brad had visited claimed knowledge of the bikini, the second of them produced a possibility. A junior saleswoman had hesitantly suggested that the deputies tried a shop called Erotica Inc., on Brook Alley in Green Valley. It seemed that the girl had been a member of Cardell University's Little Theatre group. The last play they produced before her graduation had been a version of Gypsy Rose Lee's book *The Striptease Murders*. Needing costumes, the producer – her steady boy-friend – had found a theatrical outfitter's shop called Erotica Inc. Not only had its owner, Connie Storm, hired them the costumes, but she had come down and helped with the production. From comments the owner had made, the girl thought that she might be able to assist the deputies.

'That was some show,' Brad grinned when Alice mentioned the subject of the play. 'I saw it with Sam Cuchilo – in the interests of pure art, of course.'

'What else?' Alice smiled. 'Down to the right, Brad.'

Brook Alley was a narrow street lined with cafés, bars and other business premises. Finding a parking place for their Oldsmobile, Alice and Brad studied the buildings on each side of the street, finally locating Erotica Inc.

'*This's* the place?' Brad asked.

Certainly Erotica Inc. failed to live up to its name. On one side of it was a bookstore which would have been justified in using the same title. At the other, a shop offered the latest in 'with it' clothing, hippie wigs and false beards. Their destination, however, looked like an ordinary theatrical costumiers. Its one window held three display dummies, one dressed in an Old West gambler's outfit, the second as a dancehall girl of the same period and the third wore the kind of dress Hollywood claimed Roman ladies sported when going to watch Christians being fed to the lions.

'It doesn't look so erotic to me,' Alice admitted.

'Want to take it while I browse around next door?' Brad suggested.

'You'd look like hell in anything from this side,' Alice replied, glancing at the windows of the clothing shop. 'And you're too young to be buying books at the other. Anyways, it's not erotic stimulation you want.'

'How you do talk, woman,' Brad grinned back. 'I acted like a real gentleman last night, didn't I?'

'Only because we were both too tired to do anything else,' Alice reminded him. 'Let's hope we get something here, Brad.'

The interior of the shop proved no more erotic than its display window, having only a few run-of-the-mill costumes hanging on a rack. A counter stretched across the middle of the room, with two curtain-covered openings and a door behind it. As the deputies approached the counter, a woman came through the door. She was tall, buxom, with red hair taken in a French pleat, her good-looking face carrying almost theatrical make-up.

'Don't tell me,' she said in a friendly manner. 'Let me guess. You're a couple of adagio dancers.'

'Nope,' Alice replied.

'Wrestlers then?' the woman went on, studying Brad's muscular development.

'Deputy sheriffs,' Alice corrected and showed her id. wallet.

'So who wants to win them all?'

'Are you the owner?' Alice asked.

'That's me, hon,' the woman agreed, flickering her eyes from Alice back to Brad and studying him with admiration tinged with regret at being too old to take advantage of the meeting. 'Connie Storm. You wouldn't remember me, handsome, but I was big in the good old days of burlesque. Then they got the skeleton fetish.'

'Skeleton fetish?' Alice repeated.

'For the skinny gals, hon. I bet you like them with meat on their bones, don't you, handsome?'

Brad flashed a grin at Alice and nodded. 'Yes, ma'am. You can say that I do.'

'Anyway, I'd got past it by then,' Connie sighed. 'I knew it when the down-fronters started shouting "Put it on again".' She got her laugh and went on, 'What can I do for you?'

'Did you sell this, Miss Storm?' Alice inquired, holding out the bikini in the plastic bag.

'Let's go into my office if you want to talk business,' Connie suggested. 'Say, forget the "Miss" bit, call me "Connie". Do you two have names?'

'Alice Fayde and Brad Counter, Alice introduced.

'Mind if I call you "Alice" and "Brad"? Connie asked, leading the way into her office.

'Feel free,' Alice offered, warming to the woman.

'Have a seat. Coffee, or a drink?'

'Coffee, please,' Alice answered.

While Connie poured coffee from a percolator, Alice and Brad sat at her desk. Alice took the bikini from its plastic cover and Brad looked around the room. On its walls were numerous trade photographs of striptease stars, burlesque artists and other show business personalities. Mixed among them were a few of women wearing swimsuits and calf-long boots.

'Say, are you kin to Big Andy Counter?' Connie asked, bringing cups of coffee to the desk.

'He's my pappy,' Brad replied.

'Next time you see him, ask him about the Oilmen's convention at Big D in '48,' Connie suggested with a grin.

'What happened,' Brad inquired, for he knew the Oilmen's

38

Conventions in Dallas did not attend purely to business.

'You ask your pappy,' Connie chuckled.

'Did you ever see this before, Connie?' Alice put in.

Taking the bikini, Connie gave it only a brief examination before nodding. 'Sure. I sold it.'

'Who to?'

'Well, I've sold three of them in the past week. Had them made up to a special order.'

'Who bought them?'

'One went to Zippy Sharon. She does a strip at the Queen of Clubs.'

'Is she still there?' Alice asked, for Brad had begun to look at the photographs again.

'She was last night,' Connie confirmed. 'I took her some new costumes over.'

'And the other two?'

'How important is this, Alice?'

'It's a killing.'

'That figures with Jack Tragg's folk handling it,' Connie said soberly. 'The second one went to an Upton Heights socialite who wouldn't want folks hearing that she even knew my place exists.'

'Could this belong to her?'

'It's hard to say. All three of them were the same size.'

'What colour hair has she?' Alice asked, watching Brad rise and walk across to make a closer study of the pictures.

'Natural blonde.'

'Has she a good figure?'

'She could wear the bikini and make it look good.'

'How tall is she?'

'I'd say around five-seven. She met me on The Street on Saturday to collect it. Told me her husband was taking her to Tampico on vacation on Monday. Between us girls, I don't think she cared for the notion.'

'Why?' Alice asked, throwing another glance at Brad.

'She's younger than her husband and likes to be around fellers her own age,' Connie explained.

Feeling Alice's hot glances, Brad held down a grin. To be fair to him, he was acting with the best of motives and not merely looking at pictures of scantily-clad females. His attention was centred on a young woman with medium-long black hair, wearing a one-piece swimsuit and what he saw to be boxing ring-boots. She stood with her arms raised and bent to show well-developed muscles. Under the picture was written, *'To Connie. Best wishes, Bubsy Baxter.'* The inscription did not interest Brad but the background of the picture did. The young woman stood in the corner of a boxing ring.

'Say, Alice,' Brad drawled, walking back to the desk. 'What did the m.e. tell us about the victim's physical condition?'

'That it was excellent and her muscular development remarkable,' Alice replied.

'I've just figured out a job where a girl would need muscles and have to keep her fingernails trimmed real short.'

'What job?'

'A girl wrestler.'

'It's strange you should say that,' Connie put in. 'I sold the third bikini to Fairy Manders.'

'Who's she?' Alice demanded.

'A gal grappler,' Connie replied. 'One of the best. I've seen her in action a few times. She never played Gusher City, though.'

'It could be her, Alice,' Brad said. 'How old is she, Connie?'

'Twenty-three,' the woman replied. 'A blonde and a real good looker.'

'And the socialite?' Alice asked.

'About the same. She hit the big-time as a stripper at sixteen, although she looked older. Got married two years back. Nobody around here knows about her past.'

'Then it could be either of them,' Alice remarked.

'The fingernails—' Brad began.

'N— The socialite always kept hers cut short,' Connie told him. 'And she was fit. The physical culture bit's the in thing among her set.'

'We'll have to have her name, Connie,' Alice warned. 'But we'll keep you out of it.'

'How about Fairy Manders?' Brad went on. 'When did she buy the bikini?'

'On Monday morning. She came in for it and we talked,' Connie answered. 'She's been laid off with a knee injury for

40

a month or so and was going to St. Louis to start a circuit on Tuesday.'

'How tall is she?' Alice asked.

'Five seven. She's a blonde, beautiful—' Connie replied. 'Why not? The ring-worms don't go for crows wrestling. The days are over when a promoter could toss a couple of fat old burlesque dames into a ring, or put a couple of gypsy kids together for a hair-yanking. Now the public wants good-looking, skilful dolls in the bouts. Fairy was all of that, I can tell you.'

'How well do you know her?' Alice inquired.

'She bought her ring outfits here. I deal with most of the top girls. Fancy ring jackets, matching swimsuits and boots, like that. All Tom and Bubsy Baxter's stable come here.'

'I was just looking at Bubsy's picture,' Brad remarked.

'That was before her and Tom were in a car crash. They retired from competition after it and went into promotion. Fairy's one of their girls.'

'Why was she down here in Gusher City then?'

'The Baxters have their training camp out by Calverton, She'd been resting up there.'

'Was Miss Manders alone when she came for the bikini?' Alice wanted to know.

'Sure,' Connie admitted and something in her voice drew Alice's attention.

'Was she flying to St. Louis?' Brad asked before his partner could frame her next question.

'Going by train. She had a thing about flying, wouldn't go aboard a plane, she told me.'

'Do you know if she had any boy-friends?' Alice inquired.

Connie paused for a moment, then shrugged her shoulders. 'If it is Fairy, you'll likely come to it sooner or later.'

'What?' Alice prompted.

'Fairy's a dyke – at least I think she is.'

'Why?'

'About two weeks back I saw her in a spot down here. She was with a bull-dyke* called Johnny.'

'Do you know this "Johnny's" real name?' Alice said.

* Bull-dyke: Female homosexual who plays the male role.

41

'No. She looked sort of familiar, but I can't place her. V. and G. raided the spot and padlocked it last week, they might know her.'

'Do you have a photograph of Fairy Manders?' Brad asked.

'No,' Connie admitted. 'She was going to send me one in the bikini— Say, she told me there had been an article about her in *Ring Wrestling* magazine a couple of months back.'

'Try next door and see if they've the issue with it in, Brad,' Alice suggested. 'If Connie will let me use her phone, I'll ask R. and I.* to run "Johnny" through their "monicker" file and then see if the socialite went to Tampico with her husband.'

Leaving Alice to make the calls, Brad went to the bookstore next door. He entered to find it empty. Its shelves bore piles of magazines ranging from the slick glossies which dispensed 'culture' and nudes, pin-up issues with titles like *'Busty'* or *'Slick'* offering nudes or scantily dressed females without the 'culture', to men's magazines which adroitly combined adventure with sex, for every front cover was larded with girls in various stages of undress no matter where the action be happening. Discreetly displayed at the rear were frankly erotic and bizarre publications catering for wasp-waist, high-heel, bondage, spanking and girl-fight fans.

Seeing a pile of wrestling magazines, Brad went over and picked up a copy of *Ring Wrestling*. The door at the back of the room opened. A shortish, bearded man in hippie clothes came through it followed by a burly, unshaven teenager wearing a tee-shirt, jeans and motor-cycle boots.

'We sell 'em, mac,' the teenager announced in a tough voice, stepping by his companion. 'You want to read, go to a library.'

'I'm looking f—' Brad began.

'Out and look some other place,' ordered the teenager.

'Tell hi—' Brad began.

Stepping forward, the youngster lashed a punch towards Brad. At the same moment the hippie gave a squawk of, 'No, Lennie!'

Throwing up his right hand, Brad caught the fist against

* R. and I.: Records and Identification Detail of the G.C.P.D.

his palm before it reached his face. Surprise flickered on Lennie's surly, unshaven features as Brad's powerful fingers closed over his hand and halted it progress. Before the shock wore off, Brad brought the trapped arm down. Twisting at it, he forced Lennie to turn away from him and bent the limb across the back of the tee-shirt. Then Brad gripped the scruff of Lennie's neck with his left hand and heaved the youngster back through the door. Crashing into the wall on the other side of the room beyond the door, Lennie sank to the floor in a crumpled heap.

The hippie leapt aside to avoid Lennie and darted behind the counter, his right hand dipping beneath it.

'You're getting old,' Brad told him. 'Time was when a guy like you could smell law without needing to see the tin.'

'Badge, huh?' the hippie hissed, dropping the revolver on to the shelf and jerking his empty hand into view. 'Look, I've told Lennie afore about his temper—'

'He must lose you customers,'Brad interrupted. 'And don't look so nervous. I'm from the Sheriff's Office, not Vice and Gambling. What I want is a back issue of *Ring Wrestling*.'

'So take a look for it.'

With the hippie's permission granted, Brad skimmed through the various mat magazines. Finding the August issue of *Ring Wrestling*, he opened it. Second on the list of contents was an article entitled, *'Everybody Loves Fairy Manders'*. Flipping over the pages, Brad reached the article. He bit down a low exclamation as he found a full-page photograph of the girl. If Fairy Manders was the body lying in the morgue, she had a beautiful face to match the magnificent curves.

'I'll take this,' Brad said, crossing to the counter and dropping fifty cents on it.

'It's on the house,' the hippie muttered.

'And defraud the Revenue Department, for shame?' Brad drawled, then jerked a thumb towards the moaning Lennie. 'Tell your buddie he's bad for your business.'

Nodding, the hippie scooped the fifty cent piece into the till. Then he watched the big blond leave the shop and turned to go into the back room.

Outside, Brad opened the magazine and read the article. The gist of it was that the girl was highly skilled in the ring, a 'goodie' who played to the rules even when provoked by the 'villainesses', and well-liked by all who came into contact with her.

Thinking of the body he had seen in the woods, Brad let out a low sigh. If it was Fairy Manders, somebody had not liked her at all.

CHAPTER SIX

SERGEANT JACOBS looked at the two young men standing before the reception desk in the entrance hall of the Department of Public Safety Building. A man did not spend six years riding the desk at Headquarters without developing an instinct for picking visitors who meant trouble. Unless his instinct had gone back on him, the pair before him had not come to ease the burden of some peace officer's life.

'What can I do for you?' Jacobs asked in a professionally-polite tone cultivated as desk sergeant in the house which contained the top brass of the county's law enforcement departments, so received more than its share of influential callers.

'I'm Crossman,' replied the shorter visitor, with the air of a deity announcing 'I am God'. He was a chubby, well-dressed young man whose face bore an expression of condescending superiority. 'This is Charles Richard Flaker. He came to us and confessed to the Morgan Turn-Off killing.'

Slowly Jacobs eyed Flaker from head to toe. Tall, gaunt, bearded, a hippie complete with beads, the self-confessed killer did not look an imposing specimen.

'Why'd he go to the *Mirror* instead of reporting to the nearest police house?' Jacobs inquired mildly.

'He wanted to make sure that the facts of his motivation were made public.'

Crossman's tone held cordiality. Although Sergeant Jacobs was a long-serving member of the 'Fascist' G.C.P.D., he was also Jewish. As a member of the world's second most important minority group, that made him acceptable in the reporter's intellectual eyes.

Before the sergeant could ask why Flaker felt his

45

motivation should be inflicted on the public, his attention was distracted. Alice Fayde and Brad Counter came from the rear of the building, having just parked their deputy car on returning to report their findings in Green Valley.

'Alice, Brad!' Jacobs called. 'Can you spare a minute?'

'For you, any time, Willy,' Alice smiled, coming to the desk and eyeing the two young men with distaste. 'What can I do for you?'

'Mr. Flaker here's been to the *Mirror* and confessed to the Morgan Turn-Off murder,' the sergeant explained. 'So Mr. Crossman's brought him along to us.'

A slight frown creased Crossman's brow as he looked at Jacobs. Despite the thinly veiled sarcasm in the sergeant's voice, his face showed no expression.

'You'd better come with us, Mr. Flaker,' Alice said quietly. 'We're assigned to the case.'

'I'll come along—' Crossman began.

'Not without a pass from the P.R.,' Jacobs interrupted, still annoyed that another *Mirror* reporter had tricked his way past the desk earlier and gone upstairs to pester the Sheriff's Office day watch commander.

Knowing Jacobs to be within his rights, Crossman scowled but raised no objections. Turning on his heel, he went to the Public Relations Bureau's office and asked for the required pass. Much to his annoyance, a reporter from the other local paper, the *Daily Lightning*, was in the office and asked to be included in hearing the confession.

'Take Mr. Flaker to the waiting-room, Brad,' Alice said as they left the elevator on the third floor. 'I'll go and see the watch commander.'

'Yo!' Brad replied, while Flaker looked even more worried than he had ever since leaving the reporter.

A man and woman, who had been interviewed by the Missing Persons Detail about their absent daughter, were sitting in the waiting-room. Although they looked at Brad and Flaker with interest, they did not speak. Coming to the door, a detective from Missing Persons caught Brad's brief head-shake and walked on by. Although the couple did not know it, they were now performing an important function in modern law-enforcement.

On more than one occasion, in similar circumstances,

46

young men of Flaker's type had inflicted minor injuries on themselves and later accused the arresting officer of brutality. To avoid such incidents, with the attendant bad publicity, Jack Tragg ruled that a single peace officer would only stay with a prisoner in an emergency. At all other times, the officer must have independent witnesses on hand.

The delay had its advantages for the couple. While they were kept waiting, word reached Missing Persons that the girl had returned home after a visit to an aunt and forgetting to notify her parents of doing so.

After seeing Brad safely covered by witnesses, Alice went along the passage and knocked at the watch commander's door. As she expected on being invited in, she found her immediate superior present. First Deputy McCall nodded to Alice but neither rose from the desk nor removed his hat. He meant no disrespect, for Alice forgot social conventions during watch hours and did not expect her male companions to rise when she entered a room. Nobody had ever seen McCall without his hat – not even his wife, so office rumour hinted. Big, gaunt, McCall might have posed for a picture of a Scottish highlander. He was a shrewd peace officer, tough and capable.

'Ric's filled me in on your case,' McCall said, nodding to Alvarez who was standing at the side of the desk. 'Anything else to add yet?'

'We've two possibilities for the victim. An Upton Heights socialite, but I don't buy her being the victim—'

'Who's the other?'

'A girl wrestler called Fairy Manders.'

'That figures,' McCall grunted. 'I've just read the necropsy report.'

'We could tie it to her,' Alice said. 'Call the m.e. and ask if she's had an injury to her left knee recently. If she has, it's Fairy Manders.'

'I'll do that,' McCall promised. 'The report's on your desk with the other stuff. Latent Prints have no record of her, but they've passed the prints on to I.C.R.* and the F.B.I. Sam Hellman's sent up his scene of crime shots and some of the victim after she was cleaned up. R. and I. called to say

* I.C.R.: Identification and Criminal Records Division of the Texas Department of Public Safety at Austin.

47

no make on "Johnny". Upton Heights Division came through to say the party you asked for left with her husband for Tampico on Monday afternoon.',

'Huh huh,' Alice said. 'I'll contact the Airport Detail and see if she was known to anybody down there and did fly out with her husband. And I may be able to find this "Johnny" for myself.'

'Say, Alice,' Alvarez grinned. 'When you go into the squadroom, keep your guard up. Joan Hilton's going to fix your wagon but good.'

'Why?' Alice inquired, although she knew the answer.

'Who do you reckon's been taking down all this guff for you?' the day watch commander replied. 'Say, if you pair're going to tangle, let's hire a hall. It should be a sell-out brawl.'

'She's too heavy for me,' Alice answered and got down to serious business. 'Is the sheriff in?'

'No. He's at a conference,' McCall told her. 'You getting to be a snob, Alice? Time was when Ric or me'd do.'

'Brad and I brought a guy up,' the girl replied quietly. 'He reckons that he killed our victim.'

Both the watch commanders looked hard at the girl's face. Her last piece of news ought to have been given priority. Knowing Alice to be fully aware of that, the men waited to hear what they figured would be perfectly sound reasons for the omission.

'What do you think to that?' McCall asked.

'I don't know,' Alice admitted. 'He's a hippie and looks way out. Got an anti-Vietnam button on his shirt and one for "Make Love Not War".'

'Some of the most violent cusses I know are pacifists,' McCall remarked.

'I know,' Alice agreed. 'This one went to the *Mirror* before he came here and wants to make a public confession in front of the press.'

'*Mirror*, huh?' Alvarez put in. 'They seem to be taking a lot of interest in your case, Alice.'

'How come?'

'Vassel called again just before you came in, wanting to know if there're any developments. I told him to ask P.R. Have you anything on this girl wrestler?'

'Her name's Fairy Manders. She's been out of the game with a knee injury and staying with her trainers at their place outside Calverton. I called their number but there wasn't a reply. I'll try later and see if she made St. Louis or not. Brad turned up an article in *Ring Wrestling* about her, with photographs. There's something I don't like about Flaker's confession. I don't get why he's doing it.'

'You reckon he might be a nut, confessing to work off his secret guilt bit?' McCall asked.

'I don't know,' Alice admitted. 'That was why I thought we'd do it big when we interrogate him. In the sheriff's office, with the reporters on hand, the whole bit.'

'Go make your calls while I set it up,' McCall ordered.

'And I'll set him up so he'll have a shoulder to cry on when we're through,' Alice said. 'Dick Tupman and Frank Ortega might be best.'

'They should be in by now,' McCall said, glancing at the wall clock. 'Go to it, Alice.'

On going through the connecting door into the squad-room, Alice saw the men she wanted. However Woman Deputy Joan Hilton came towards her before she could address the Negro and Mexican deputies.

'You should hire a secretary,' the rubbery, buxom, good-looking blonde remarked. 'I've emptied two ball-point pens taking down your calls.'

'Make a switch then,' Alice suggested cheerfully.

'Like how?' Joan asked suspiciously.

'Call Calverton one-three-one for me.'

'Can do. I've two minutes and twenty-seven seconds left of my watch and I may as well spend them profitably.'

'Can you relieve Brad, Tommy?' Alice asked a Chinese deputy who stood at the bulletin board. 'He's got a suspect in the waiting-room.'

'Sure,' Deputy Chu replied. 'For you, anything.'

'You'll have Pat Rafferty after your hide,' Joan warned from the desk where she sat dialling the Calverton number.

A convention had grown in the squadroom, with Chu's Irish partner asking Alice to marry him daily, despite already having a wife and family.

By the time Brad came from the waiting-room, Joan had told Alice there was no answer from her call. So Alice said

49

she would try later and explained to Brad what was planned.

'I showed him Fairy Manders' photograph in *Ring Wrestling* accidental-like,' Brad remarked, taking the magazine from his jacket pocket. 'He didn't do anything or say he knew her.'

'Put it in the folder with the other stuff,' Alice replied. 'We'll let him stew in his own juice for a while longer, then make a start.'

On their desk lay the various reports and an official envelope. Alice tipped out its contents. Top of the pile of photographs was a close-up of the victim's face in all its hideous detail. She checked the pile quickly and returned them to the envelope. Then she called the Airport Detail of the G.C P.D., asking about the socialite and was promised a speedy reply. Dialling again, she made a reservation for a manicure later in the evening. Just as she finished, McCall appeared at the connecting door.

'Everything's set up,' the watch commander announced. 'All we want is the star performer.'

'I'll get him,' Brad promised.

'Can you stand by to help with a sympathetic shoulder, Dick, Frank?' Alice asked as the two deputies came to their desk.

'Sure,' the Negro grinned. 'We've the softest shoulders in town. What's up, Alice?'

Leaving Alice to explain, Brad returned to the waiting-room and motioned Chu to bring Flaker out.

'He-all been giving you any trouble Tom?' Brad asked, his southern drawl even more pronounced and jerking Flaker's eyes to his face.

'No,' Chu answered.

'Now ain't that a pity,' Brad said, driving his right fist into the left palm with a hard, smacking sound. 'Yes sir, Tommy boy, that's a real pity.'

'Take it easy, Brad!' Chu put in, sounding nervous. 'You know what happened last time!'

'You hush your flapping mouth about last time, you hear me!' Brad growled. ' 'Twarn't nothing but an accident that could've happened to anybody. Anyways, the County Commissioners never heard tell of it.'

A worried, frightened expression came to Flaker's face.

Suddenly he became aware that there were no independent witnesses, the man and woman still being in the waiting-room.

'I didn't mean anything, Brad,' Chu stated, darting nervous glances around. 'Only I don't want to be inv—'

'Go back to the squadroom then,' Brad sneered. 'Tain't but a step to the boss's office and I can tend his needings until we get there.'

While Chu almost scuttled back into the squadroom, Brad shoved the left side of his jacket to let the big black butt of the automatic show prominently. Flaker kept as far as he could from the big, blond deputy during the short walk along the passage. Just as they reached the door to Jack Tragg's office, Brad came to a halt. Placing his right hand against the wall in front of Flaker, he glared coldly into the hippie's scared face.

'Listen good to me, feller,' Brad growled. 'We're going to be asking you-all some questions in there. Make sure that you give the right answers – or you and me're set for a lil talk on our lonesome later.'

CHAPTER SEVEN

FLAKER showed some relief on being taken into the sheriff's office, despite the law being present in strength. It seemed unlikely that they would use physical violence against him with Crossman of the *Mirror* in the room. Alice led Flaker to a chair alongside the sheriff's desk, then ranged herself by Alvarez in front of the hippie. Brad moved forward to stand at McCall's side, the four of them making a half-circle about Flaker. A police stenographer sat at the desk, pen poised over an imposing notebook, ready to take down the conversation.

'Something bothering you, Mr. Flaker?' McCall inquired.

'Where're the television cameras?' the hippie muttered.

'We want to hear what you have to say first,' the big Scot answered. 'You've got reporters here from the *Mirror* and *Lightning*, so your motivation'll reach the public.'

Which was not what Flaker had hoped for, but a glance at Brad caused him to accept the terms. After learning Flaker's full name and address, Alice opened the questioning.

'What's your occupation, Mr. Flaker?'

'I'm temporarily unemployed.'

'How long have you been "temporarily" unemployed?'

'For four years.'

'And before that?'

'I was at the University of North Texas. I majored in Economics.'

'So you've never had a job?'

'No,' Flaker admitted surlily.

'Why did you kill her, Flaker!'

The words cracked from Alvarez's lips, jerking Flaker's attention from the gentle-speaking Alice. A trickle of sweat ran down the hippie's face and he ran his tongue tip across his lips. Nothing was happening as he figured it should.

From all appearances, the peace officers were prepared to give him a gruelling interrogation.

'I – I met her in a bar—' Flaker finally answered, darting a glance in Crossman's direction.

'When?' Brad barked.

'Mon— on Monday evening.'

'What was her name?' Alice snapped in a tone very different from that used during her first questions.

'I – I don't know!' Flaker croaked. 'Betty – she said – I didn't get her other name.'

'Do you always kill strangers?' McCall growled.

'I never— I only killed the girl!'

'Where did you meet her?' Alvarez demanded.

'A – At the Peace Inn, in Green Valley, I think.'

'You don't know?' Alice asked.

'Yes. It was the Peace Inn. We had a couple of drinks and went—'

'What time was this?' the girl snapped.

'Er— About ten. We got in her car and drove along Route 118, then along the Morgan Turn-Off.'

'Why'd you kill her?' Alvarez asked.

'We got talking. She said she was a member of the National Fascist Party,' Flaker answered, sounding more certain and confident than previously. 'Kept saying how we should run out all the kikes, niggers and greasers. The way she talked got me. All I could see was pictures of what happened at Belsen and Dachau—'

'Where did the gun come from?' McCall interrupted.

'The gu—' Flaker faltered, then he started to speak clearly again. 'I bought it and the ammunition from a hock-shop in the Bad Bit. You know how easy it is to buy a gun. If it hadn't been, I couldn't have killed that girl.'

For the first time during the questioning, Crossman's pen moved across his note-pad. The *Lightning* reporter had been taking down everything that was said. After glancing at Crossman, the other newspaperman gave a faint grin.

'What time did you kill her?' Brad asked.

'Half past ten or so. But I couldn't have—'

'Where are her clothes?' Alice cut in.

'I – I burned them and threw the ashes in the Rio Grande,' Flaker muttered.

'And the gun?' McCall went on.

'I threw it away down by the river. I've no idea where.'

'Why did you decide to surrender, Mr. Flaker?' Crossman inquired.

'We'll ask the questions!' Alvarez barked. 'What did you do with the empty cartridge cases, Flaker?'

'Empty—?' the hippie gulped.

'That were ejected from the gun!' Alvarez continued. 'Don't you know anything about guns?'

Once more Flaker showed no hesitation in replying. 'Of course I know about guns. Ever since I was old enough to carry one, my father let me go shooting. I've killed rabbits, birds, deer. That's where I learned how to shoot so I could ki—'

The words died off as Flaker watched McCall pull a revolver from under his jacket. Turning so that the suspect could not see his actions, the First Deputy tipped free the cylinder of his Smith & Wesson Model 27 revolver and ejected its six, long, flat-nosed .357 Magnum bullets. After showing the others the empty chambers, he closed the cylinder, gripped the three-and-a-half inch barrel and held the gun butt forward towards Flaker.

'Show us, on Deputy Fayde here, how you shot the woman.'

For a self-confessed killer, Flaker showed a remarkable reluctance to help the peace officers. Making no attempt to take the revolver, he threw an imploring look at Crossman.

'Is this all necessary?' Crossman demanded.

'We think so,' McCall stated. 'It's important we know all the facts before we bring a charge of murder against Mr. Flaker.'

'It's a trick to get my fingerprints!' Flaker croaked, suggesting a motive calculated to appeal to the *Mirror* reporter.

'Why'd we bother with tricks?' Alvarez scoffed. 'And if we did, we'd use something better than a gun with First Deputy McCall's prints all over it.'

'I've a sketch in here, made up by our firearms experts,' Alice explained to the reporters, indicating the folder. 'It shows the angles at which the bullets entered the victim's body. We'd like to check its accuracy with Mr. Flaker's help.'

'That sounds reasonable enough to me,' the *Lightning's* representative said.

'But he's already confessed to the killing,' Crossman objected, meaning to carry on with a demand that the brow-beating and persecution was ended.

'And we want to make sure of the facts,' McCall pointed out. 'Of course, if he doesn't want to co-operate, we'll take him down and book him right now.'

Realizing that would end his chance of explaining his 'motivation' to the press, Flaker stood up and reluctantly took the revolver from McCall. Then he turned to face Alice and began to point the barrel at her.

'How about the safety catch?' Brad said in a disgusted tone.

By that time Flaker was alert for tricks. Thinking desperately, he remembered reading an *87th Precinct* novel where the detective checked that his revolver's safety catch was applied. Figuring that he might be committing a blunder, he looked down at the 'maggie'. Sure enough, there was a square-shaped catch on the left side at the rear of the cylinder. Seeing nothing else that even vaguely resembled a safety catch, he pressed the protuberance with his thumb – and the cylinder tipped out.

'So you've handled guns all your life, have you?' McCall said dryly, taking back the revolver.

'Ye— Yes,' Flaker insisted. 'But not that type.'

'What type then?' Brad snapped.

'A – A Colt.'

'Revolver or automatic?' Alice demanded.

'A revolver,' Flaker told her.

'What model?' Brad snapped.

'Wha— How would I know what model?' Flaker squealed. 'I bought the gun second-hand, without needing a permit or—'

'What did you do with the empty cases that were ejected as you shot her?' Alvarez repeated and the *Lightning* reporter sat watching Flaker with extra interest.

'I – I picked them up and threw them into the Rio Gr—' Flaker began.

'Revolvers don't eject their bullets, Flaker!' Alvarez

55

shouted, moving closer to the man. 'And they don't have safety catches, either!'

Silence dropped on the room after the announcement. Crouching down in his chair, Flaker glared wildly from face to face. He had expected his 'confession' to be all the peace officers needed, believing they would be only too pleased to have the case over. Instead they had put him through an intense interrogation, giving him no chance to make his imposing speeches. It almost seemed that they were trying to prove him innocent, not guilty.

At last McCall broke the silence. Looming over Flaker, the big First Deputy eyed him with an air of loathing and growled, 'Do you know what you are, Flaker?'

'A murderer,' the hippie insisted in a whining voice. 'But I wouldn't have been if there had been restrictions on the pur—'

'So you're a murderer, are you?' Alvarez interrupted.

'Yes. But only because of the ease with whi—'

While Flaker spoke, Alice opened the folder. She took out the photograph of the victim's head before it had been cleaned up by the m.e.

'And this's what you did to her!' Alice hissed, thrusting the photograph in the hippie's direction.

Flaker glanced down, then stiffened in his seat with eyes bulging out and face twisting in an expression of nausea. No sound left his lips, but he tried to move backwards as Alice brought the sheet of glossy paper nearer to his face.

'You killed her and did this?' Alice repeated, voice throbbing with loathing.

'I – I—!' Flaker gasped.

'You're not a killer, Flaker!' McCall roared. 'You're nothing but a damned liar – and an inefficient liar at that.'

Slamming his chair back against the wall, Crossman leapt to his feet. 'There's no need for these Gest—'

Something in McCall's dour face as he turned to face the reporter brought the words to an end.

'This cr— man didn't kill her,' Alvarez stated flatly.

'I did so ki—!' Flaker whined.

'Don't for god's sake try to snow us!' McCall roared. 'Did you reckon we'd be dumb enough to fall for your phoney confession and sit back cheering while you spouted anti-gun propaganda?'

'You've no right to—' Crossman yelped, trying to assert his intellectual superiority and defence of the under-dog.

'Right!' McCall spat out the word. He snatched the photograph from Alice's hand, then stalked across the room to hold it in front of Crossman's face. *'Right?* Some lousy nut does this to a woman and you sit there saying I've no right to call down a cheap hippie crud who comes here wasting our time with his phoney confession.'

For a moment Crossman stared with widening, horrified eyes at the photograph. Then he let out a strangled squawk, turned and stumbled to the door. Jerking it open, he plunged through and staggered blindly along the passage to the Men's room at the other end.

'Do you want to look at it?' McCall growled at the *Lightning* reporter.

'Not after what it did to Crossman,' he replied, closing the notebook in which he had been writing all through the interrogation. Then he nodded to where Flaker cowered in the chair. 'That lousy creep. I've seen some sorry specimens in my time, but, man, he's the end.'

'Get him out of here, Brad!' Alvarez ordered.

'I – I don't say another word until I've seen a lawyer!' Flaker mumbled.

'Take him to the interrogation rooms, Brad,' Alvarez repeated.

'On your feet, crud!' Brad ordered and the snarl in his voice brought instant obedience. 'Get moving.'

'Go with them, friend,' McCall suggested to the reporter.

The affair might still be worked into a charge of ' police brutality', so the First Deputy took steps to avoid it. Nodding his agreement, the reporter followed Brad and Flaker from the office and along to the special interrogation room.

Designed to protect the suspect and investigating officers, the interrogation rooms were divided into two unequal parts. The outer compartment was small and had seats for two witnesses, being separated from the inner by a soundproof glass sliding door. Witnesses could see everything done in the second compartment, while unable to hear what was said; the idea being to prevent abuses by the officers, or false accusations against them.

'I can make a phone call,' Flaker announced as Brad closed the glass door behind them, taking heart from seeing the *Lightning* reporter in the other section.

'After we've charged you,' Brad answered. 'Now clam up. That guy won't be around all the time.'

'I – I won't say another word!' Flaker insisted, glancing to make sure that the man – who worked for a newspaper he normally regarded with all his bigoted hatred as being an organ of the grasping capitalists – was still watching.

'Conversation's the last thing I want with you,' Brad stated and leaned against the wall, idly cracking his right fist into the palm of his left hand.

Five minutes dragged by. During that time Brad never took his eyes off Flaker's face. The hippie grew increasingly nervous, wondering what his fate would be when the deputy got him alone. Then the outer door of the rooms opened. Deputy Tupman entered, followed by his partner, Deputy Ortega, carrying a tray with a coffee-pot and cups on it. Both deputies now wore their uniforms and Tupman had a sergeant's chevrons on his sleeves.

'We'll take over now, Counter,' the Negro declared as they came into the inner room and closed the door.

'Sure,' Brad muttered in a surly tone.

Before Brad could leave, Tupman's voice lashed at him. 'Sure – what?'

'Sure – sergeant!' Brad answered in a more sullen tone; just as Flaker expected a nigger-hating Southerner to react to a Negro who outranked him.

'Has that peckerwood* been giving you a bad time, friend?' Tupman asked Flaker after Brad angrily left the room.

'Here, have a cup of coffee, *amigo*,' Ortega continued in an amiable manner.

Letting out a sigh of relief, Flaker relaxed. A Negro and Mexican, being members of minority groups, would be more understanding than the Fascist brutes who grilled him.

'Now, friend,' Tupman said kindly, taking a seat facing Flaker. 'What's it all about?'

Half an hour later Tupman entered the deputies' squad-

* Peckerwood: Negro's derogatory name for a white Southerner.

58

room. The Negro grinned at the 'nigger-hating' Southerner.

'He's talked up a storm, Brad. Sobbed bitter tears all over our sympathetic shoulders,' Tupman said.

'He's one of those anti-gun cranks, is he?' Brad replied, showing none of his previous hostility.

'Just as cranky as they come. He reckons he thought confessing would be good anti-gun publicity and that the law wouldn't mind if he helped to have the ownership of firearms stopped. Why the hell do these crud always think every badge wants to stop honest folks owning guns?'

'It gives their ego a boost that way,' Brad guessed. 'How'd the *Mirror* get involved in it?'

'He wanted press coverage and thought they'd be the best folks to give it. Way he says it, Crossman left him alone in his office and there was our P.R. handout on the desk. Flaker read it and learned enough to convince Crossman he'd done the killing.'

'Not that Crossman'd want much convincing,' Brad said.

'We can't prove he knew Flaker was lying, though,' Tupman replied. 'Way he'll tell it, he was just a reporter doing his job.'

Brad nodded, guessing what had happened. Probably Crossman knew Flaker was a liar and deliberately left him where he could pick up enough details to make his story sound more plausible. Then the reporter brought the hippie along, ready to make capital out of his anti-gun protestations.

The very fact that Flaker went first to the *Mirror* had aroused Alice's suspicions. Men of Flaker's type hated firearms, mainly because people who enjoyed shooting mostly held political views in opposition to their own, and the *Mirror* continually blazed out demands for restrictions on gun ownership. So Alice arranged the by-play to draw out the truth.

Knowing Flaker's kind believed all peace officers took delight in beating up prisoners, Brad and Tommy Chu began the process with veiled hints of a mythical incident. Although they made no mention of what the incident had been, Flaker suspected the worst. The grilling in Jack Tragg's office and the grim menace of Brad's presence in the interrogation room further built up to an atmosphere which made

Flaker susceptible when offered a shoulder to cry on. For a man with Flaker's mentality, Tupman – a Negro, currently the intellectual's number one under-dog – and Ortega had been the deputies most likely to appeal to him as sympathetic listeners.

Brad's surly attitude when addressing Tupman in the interrogation room had also been part of the act. So had the Negro donning a sergeant's stripes, relying on Flaker not knowing that a deputy sheriff out-ranked a sergeant. There was no racial distrust between the deputies. On occasion Brad had worked alongside Tupman, without a thought of colour. For his part, Tupman had not hesitated to put his life in Brad's hands when dealing with a dangerous criminal; even though intellectuals like Flaker believed every Negro hated and distrusted Southerners.

McCall came through the connecting door and looked at Tupman. 'Did you nail him, Dick?'

'We've got enough for obstructing an investigation,' the Negro replied. 'When Frank took him upstairs he was sobbing down my shirt about how *the* President would still be alive and steering the country in the right direction if there was restriction on the purchase of guns.'

'Now I've got the bastard!' McCall barked. 'It's been bugging me since I first saw him.'

'What's that, Mac?' Tupman inquired.

'Where I knew him from,' McCall replied. 'He was one of the leaders of a "Kennedy is a war-monger" march during the Cuban confrontation.'

'That's just his damned bigoted kind's way,' Brad growled. 'From war-monger to *the* President. I often wonder if they'd have been so set on proving Oswald innocent if he'd been right-wing instead of a commie?'

Before the debate could go farther, the telephone on Brad's desk buzzed. As the big blond went to it, McCall looked at Tupman and asked if he was free.

'As a bird,' the Negro replied.

'You and Frank'd best roll down to 79 Memphis Street. There's been a knifing in a crap game. Local boys have it in hand, but you'd best take a look.'

'That's one of the evils of gambling, brother,' Tupman drawled, rolling his eyes heavenwards in the manner of a hot-gospel preacher. 'Me and Frank'll go down and spread the good word to the heathens.'

'Hallelujah!' Brad called, raising the receiver to his ear. 'Sheriff's Office. Yeah, me, Alice. No, Dick's just trying to save our souls. For shame, and you such a pleasant-talking gal most times.' Then he listened to the rest of his partner's words. 'I'll be down. The Airport Detail called to say the socialite left with her husband, she's known down there. Anyways, the m.e. came through. The victim had had a recent injury to her left knee. Yeah, Alice. It's Fairy Manders.'

'What'd Alice say?' McCall inquired as Brad hung up. 'I mean the parts fit for a married man to hear.'

'She's got a lead on the bull-dyke, Johnny,' Brad replied. 'Wants me to pick her up and we'll go see the lady – or gent, depends on how you look at it.'

CHAPTER EIGHT

THE killer of Fairy Manders sat in a grey Ford Sedan and looked across Randel Street at the entrance to the Department of Public Safety Building. Although he tried to tell himself there was no way in which the killing could be brought home to him, he still felt nagging doubts. Much as he hated to admit it, the Sheriff's Office deputies were efficient and thorough in their work.

Yet there seemed to be no way that the deputies might identify his victim. He had smashed her face beyond recognition. The dress, coat, shoes and handbag she wore on the fatal date had been destroyed and disposed of irrecoverably. To the best of his knowledge, Fairy had never been in trouble with the law. So her fingerprints would not be on record. Only the bikini remained. He should have removed and destroyed it along with her other belongings. However he had been too sick to face the prospect of bending over the hideous, ruined body and stripping the brief garments from it.

For a moment the killer sat rigid, shutting his eyes. He shook his head from side to side, as if trying to blot out the memory of how the girl had looked after he finished working on her with the revolver's barrel and butt, then burned off her hair to make identification even more difficult.

With a shudder, the killer threw off the memory. That had been Monday night and here it was Thursday, with the body discovered and the investigation begun. He wondered if the deputies could trace Fairy through the bikini. Unlikely, he decided. Those leopard print outfits were popular and she may not have bought it in Rockabye County. Even if she had, he doubted if the deputies would find the right store; or, if they did, that the person who made the sale would know Fairy. She had never been on a bill in Gusher City and looked nothing like the popular conception of a woman wrestler.

A good-looking, red-haired girl left the D.P.S. Building, crossed the street and halted a short distance from the killer's car. Even as he reached for the ignition key, she signalled to a passing taxi. The killer watched her, a puzzled frown on his face. That was Woman Deputy Alice Fayde, a member of the watch on duty at the Sheriff's Office. She worked with that big playboy, Brad Counter, but he did not accompany her.

Watching Alice enter the cab, the killer started his car's engine. From what he had heard, Fayde and Counter were handling the Manders' case. Thinking she might be going to investigate a lead, he decided to follow her. A smart man always tried to keep ahead of the opposition. Knowing what line the deputies were following might be handy.

While following Alice's taxi, the killer wondered why she was travelling without her partner. Usually deputies worked in pairs, but there was no sign of Brad Counter.

In a moment of near-panic, the killer wondered if they suspected and meant to trap him. Then his self-assurance reasserted control. There was no way the law could connect him to Fairy Manders.

At last the taxi halted, before a fashionable beautician's salon on Baines Avenue, and Alice stepped out. Bringing his car to a stop by a parking meter, the killer watched her pay the driver and enter the salon. For the first time, the killer noticed she was carrying a folded magazine of some kind. Ignoring the meter, he left his car and crossed the sidewalk. Looking through the glass doors, he saw Alice at the reception desk and being directed into one of the manicurists' booths.

A snort of indignation left the killer's lips. After taking time and trouble to trail the deputy, he found she was doing no more than grabbing a manicure. Feeling both annoyed and amused, the killer turned from the door. Something ought to be done to stop peace officers goofing off while they were supposed to be on watch and drawing their salary from the tax-payers' – his own if it came to that – money.

Just as the killer turned, he saw a patrolman approaching and realized that he had not paid the parking fee. The last thing the killer wanted was to be handed a parking ticket. So he hurried back to the car, climbed in and drove off. His actions aroused the patrolman's suspicions. Halting by the meter, the harness bull saw that no fee had been recorded for the past thirty minutes, and he knew the car had not been there ten minutes earlier. He was a rookie, young and ambitious. An older hand would have shrugged the matter off, but not him. Taking a note of the Ford's number, he later telephoned the Department of Motor Vehicles and requested a make on the owner.

The killer had just committed his first major mistake.

Inside the salon, Alice sat back in a chair unaware of how close she had been to the killer. The girl attending to Alice's nails was small, with a beautiful face and exquisite curves. While she would attract male attention in any company, it meant nothing to her. Maggie Bannion was a lesbian.

'Johnny, Miss Fayde?' she said, in answer to Alice's question. 'Do you know any more about her?'

'No.'

'I only know one "Johnny",' Maggie admitted, 'and I don't know her real name.'

'Does she go around with this girl?' Alice asked, opening the *Ring Wrestling* at Fairy Manders' picture.

'I don't think so. She goes steady with a girl we call Fluffy,' Maggie replied. 'W – Wait a minute though. Johnny and Fluffy split up a couple of weeks back. I heard Johnny got into a fight over some new girl.'

'A fight?' Alice said. 'Do you mean an argument?'

'No. A for-real fist-fight.'

'Who won?'

'I don't know. It was a bad fight before they were separated.'

'Where can I find Johnny?'

'She's mostly at the Brown Hat. It's a small place on the alley between the Gerard Theatre and the Blue Moon Tavern down on The Street.'

'How about the guy she had the fight with?' Alice asked.

'I don't know who she was,' Maggie admitted. 'You won't make any trouble at the Brown Hat, will you, Miss Fayde? It's a nice place and we're the only people who use it.'

'All I want to do is talk with Johnny,' Alice assured her. 'Get me a telephone in here, please Maggie.'

Like every deputy and detective, Alice had her small

circle of regular informers. All of Alice's band except Maggie had specialized knowledge of female criminals. Maggie knew no women crooks, her usefulness came when Alice needed information about a lesbian who was otherwise honest and law-abiding.

Maggie owed Alice a favour and occasionally supplying information was the way in which she repaid it. While working undercover for the Narcotics Detail, Alice had found Maggie on the verge of being blackmailed into acting as a pusher for the drugs. At some risk to herself, Alice saved the girl and helped break up the drug ring. She came out of the affair with promotion to woman deputy and gained Maggie's gratitude.

Coming alone to see the girl did not imply a lack of trust in Brad. Alice knew that Maggie would never talk with a man present. On leaving the salon at the completion of her manicure, she found Brad waiting in Unit SO 12 and looking like a husband whose wife had kept him hanging around.

'Head for The Street!' Alice ordered, climbing into the Oldsmobile's front seat. 'What happened after I left?'

While driving, Brad gave Alice the details and the news that Fairy Manders seemed certain to be the victim. Then Alice told what she had learned. They agreed that the lesbian called Johnny had possibilities as a suspect.

The Street once had another name, but few Gusher City folk could remember what it had been. In the days just after World War II, when Gusher City bore a reputation as a wild wide-open town, The Street had been a neon-lit dollar-trap that only rarely closed. In addition to two luxury cinemas and a theatre, there had been night clubs which offered all forms of gambling as an added attraction and cabarets calculated to bring a blush to the cheeks of a Parisian café-owner. Bars, slot-machine arcades in the alleys and streets branching from The Street offered girls, narcotics, anything a visitor might ask for, while tiny bookstores displayed pornographic literature openly.

Then returning veterans decided to clean up their home town. Jack Tragg and Phineas Hagen, now Gusher City's able chief of police, fought a hard, savage and dangerous battle. They won, driving the criminal element out. Gambling had been made illegal, the night clubs forced to clean up their shows. The back alleys were no longer blatant vice traps.

For all that, The Street lived. It was still the entertainment centre of the town. Only a few isolated voices bewailed the passing of the 'good old days'.

Leaving their car in the Gerard Theatre's parking lot, Alice and Brad walked along the alley. They found the Brown Hat, a small bar, with no difficulty but Alice decided to go in alone.

'Wait here, Brad,' she said.

'If you yell for help, I'll go find a cop,' he promised.

'That's my partner. Noble to the end,' Alice smiled and crossed the street to enter the bar.

Outwardly the Brown Hat seemed little different from dozens of other bars in Gusher City. Its lights were far from bright, but that did not appear to bother the half-a-dozen or so couple seated at tables around the room. Behind the bar, a big, heavily-built woman with shoulders and arms a strong man might have envied studied Alice with cold eyes.

'Is Johnny here?' Alice asked, going to the bar.

'Says which?' croaked the woman huskily.

'Says this,' Alice answered and flashed her id. wallet. 'Which's Johnny?'

'You're new around here—'

'You didn't look close enough. It says deputy sheriff, not detective.'

Clearly the woman knew the subtle difference. The Sheriff's Office rarely interfered with matters under the jurisdiction of the Vice and Gambling Detail of the G.C.P.D. Deputies were, however, the city's homicide squad. A mixture of worry and relief showed on the woman's face. Her eyes flickered to one of the couples, then back to Alice.

'Johnny who?'

'Don't waste both our time,' Alice said coldly. 'I don't give a damn that they're dragging in here. I want to see Johnny.'

'She ain't here,' the woman growled.

'Then I'll wait for her. And if she doesn't come in tonight, I'll have this place staked out until she shows.'

Only for a moment did the woman hesitate, for she knew what such a stake-out would do to her business.

'That's Johnny, over by the jukebox,' she muttered.

Crossing the room, Alice studied the couple at the table. The figure with its back to her wore a well-tailored man's business suit and had very short black hair. Despite the man's shirt and club tie, the features proved to be female. The other occupant of the table was a pretty, chubby brunette and looked about as feminine as a woman could get. A good-looking, intelligent face which seemed vaguely familiar looked first at Alice, then down to her open id. wallet.

'I'm Woman Deputy Fayde,' Alice said. 'Are you Johnny?'

'I'm Johnny,' the bull-dyke answered in a deep, cultured voice.

Opening the copy of *Ring Wrestling*, Alice dropped Fairy Manders' picture on to the table. Although Johnny gave no hint of recognition, the brunette gasped and fluttered a hand to her mouth.

'Do you know her?' Alice asked.

'I've never seen her before,' Johnny replied.

'Have you, Miss—?' Alice inquired, looking at the brunette.

'Fluffy's never seen her before either!' Johnny snapped.

'Let her answer, please.'

'I said she'd—'

'Here or at the Sheriff's Office,' Alice interrupted. 'It's all one to me.'

'Do you think you can take me in?' Johnny hissed, clenching her right hand.

'I've a partner outside,' Alice answered, apparently ignoring the fist but ready to meet any attack. 'He stands six foot three and weighs one ninety-five. I'm black belt at judo and brown at karate, so I reckon I can last until he comes.'

Glaring into Alice's eyes, Johnny struggled for mastery. Suddenly the brunette shot out a hand to catch Johnny's sleeve. A scared expression crossed Fluffy's face and she gasped:

'Don't do it, Johnny. Hasn't she caused you enough grief—'

'Bag your head!' Johnny snapped.

'And you use yours!' Alice barked. 'Do you reckon the rest of the folks in here'll back your play while they're in drag? Make a fuss for me and this place'll be padlocked before midnight. There's another thing for *you* to consider.'

'What's that?' Johnny asked sullenly.

'Publicity.'

Face becoming an expressionless mask, Johnny opened her hand and relaxed on the chair. While she accepted being a lesbian and saw nothing wrong with dressing in drag – wearing male clothing – she knew how news of her being a bull-dyke would affect her career.

'All right,' she said. 'I know Fairy Manders.'

'When did you see her last?' Alice inquired.

'Not since Wednesday, last week that is.'

'I understand you are friendly with her?'

'Yes—' Johnny began, but Fluffy made a disapproving noise. 'All right, we aren't friends any more. Sit down, for god's sake, you're attracting attention.'

Glancing around, Alice saw that – despite how some of the customers dressed – only women occupied the room. She saw that they were looking her way with interest, and sat down.

'I heard you used to go around together,' Alice remarked.

'What's happened to Fairy?' Johnny hissed, suspicion flickering in her eyes.

'Should anything have happened to her?' Alice countered.

'I didn't get up there by sleeping with the board of directors. Give me credit for some brains. A deputy sheriff doesn't come asking questions about—'

'Yes?' Alice prompted as the words trailed off.

'Is Fairy dead?'

'She is. Where were you on Monday night?'

'Here early on, with Fluffy. Then I changed in the back room and we went to the Blue Moon to see the new floor show. I had a table booked and we were there until midnight.'

'What name did you book the table under?'

'My own, of course.'

'And that is?'

Johnny stared at Alice with a mixture of anger and admiration. Then she slapped a hand on the table top and laughed.

'That was a neat bluff pretending you knew me. If you ever want a good job—'

'I'll keep it in mind,' Alice smiled. 'Your name, please.'

'Sarah Matburn – does any of this have to come out?'

'Not if your alibi checks,' Alice replied, studying Johnny's face and recognizing the resemblance to photographs of one of the city's most influential career women.

'I wear a wig and make-up around the company,' Johnny explained, reading Alice's thoughts. 'And my alibi will hold up. Have a drink?'

'Not while I'm on watch,' Alice answered. 'And after midnight?'

'We took the folks I'd been entertaining to my place, they left around three in the morning.'

'I hear you had a fight over Fairy,' Alice said. 'What started it?'

'Oh that,' Johnny sniffed. 'Fluffy and I had quarrelled and I went to this drum in Green Valley. I don't know why I bothered, but I was getting stoned when Fairy came in. We started talking and this guy tried to move in. She'd tried to cut in between Fluffy and me a couple of times and I was drunk enough to figure on stopping her. So we started slugging. The bartender split us out and Fairy offered to drive me home. After that we used to see each other. You know, from the start I couldn't tell if she was one of us, or just putting me on.'

'Why did you break up?'

'Last Wednesday I decided to find out which and took her to a place I have in Leander. There was some wrestling on the television and she insisted we watched it. There was a girls' bout. I didn't know Fairy was one of them and started giving out how it was all a big fakeroo.'

'Then what happened?' Alice inquired.

'She bounced out of her chair and grabbed me,' Johnny answered ruefully. 'Yelled, "So we couldn't fight our way out of a wet paper bag, huh?" and started throwing me around the room. Listen, I can handle myself. But she took me like Grant took Richmond, had me yelling "uncle" and walked out leaving me flatter than a pancake. That was the last I ever saw of Fairy Manders – or wanted to.'

'Johnny was with me all Monday,' Fluffy put in. 'I mean after the others left.'

'Huh huh,' Alice replied. 'Who was the guy you had the fight with?'

'Her name's Phyllis Congreen,' Johnny replied. 'She's a master sergeant out at the Euclid air base. I haven't seen her around since the fight.'

'What kind of person was Fairy Manders?'

'A nice kid, pleasant. Didn't talk much about herself. She was good fun – but I don't know if she was one of us,' Johnny replied. 'My company could use a girl as smart as you.'

'So can the Sheriff's Office,' Alice smiled and stood up.

'Say,' Johnny remarked, also smiling. 'Aren't you forgetting to tell me not to leave town?'

'I wouldn't insult your intelligence,' Alice answered. 'Which is in return for the compliment and the offer of a job.'

'Hey, deputy,' the bartender said as Alice walked towards the door. 'How does this leave me?'

'Still standing behind the bar,' Alice told her and left.

Going through the door, Alice saw Brad standing talking with a good-looking exceptionally well-developed girl whose blouse and mini-skirt left little to the imagination.

'Hi there, handsome,' the girl said. 'I'm available.'

'And I'm a badge,' Brad replied.

'So I give reductions for the boys in blue.'

'Let's wait and hear what my partner thinks,' Brad grinned.

'If he's like yo—' the girl began.

'Hi, Mabel,' Alice greeted, crossing the street. 'You're out early tonight.'

Turning, the girl looked Alice over and grinned. 'Hello, Miss Fayde,' she replied. 'They do say the early bird catches the worm.'

'Sure,' Alice agreed. 'But I need this worm for bait.'

'*You're* his partner?' Mabel asked.

'Yep,' Alice agreed. 'Make with the feet, worm. And he won't be taking a rain check, Mabel, so don't raise your hopes.'

Watching Alice and Brad walk off in the direction of

The Street, Mabel gave an indignant sniff. She felt there ought to be a law to prevent the wicked waste of giving such a handsome hunk of man to a female fuzz. Sure it was Mabel's job, but she had never heard of anybody being jailed for trying to enjoy their work. That big blond looked like he would make any gal happy.

'You found Johnny?' Brad inquired, after cussing Alice out for ruining his chances and receiving a promise that she would make up for it later.

'Sure. She's given me an alibi. Let's go check it out.'

CHAPTER NINE

'Johnny's alibi checks,' Alice told McCall as they stood by her team's desk in the squadroom. 'She was at the Blue Moon until midnight. If she left her apartment after three o'clock, we can't find proof of it.'

'She didn't use her car if she left,' Brad went on. 'The garage is under the apartment building and has a watchman on duty all night. He's an ex-cop and I don't reckon he was lying.'

The time was nine o'clock. Alice and Brad had just returned from investigating Johnny's alibi. Only Deputy Rafferty of the watch was in the squadroom when they entered, but McCall joined them from his office to hear of their progress.

'Fluffy has a car, but it was in her folks' garage all Monday,' Alice continued. 'I called a friend on the W.A.C. air police at Euclid. Master Sergeant Congreen was transferred to Hawaii on Friday.'

'Talking of calls,' Brad remarked, picking up their phone's receiver. 'I'll try the Baxters at Calverton again.'

Even as Brad started to dial the number, McCall's telephone buzzed. Entering his office, he scooped up the receiver.

'McCall here,' he said. 'Again?' After listening, he covered the mouthpiece with his hand. 'It's yon *Mirror* reporter, Vassel. Wants to know if we have anything on the Morgan Turn-Off killing. Shall I tell him we've identified her?'

'I'd rather we kept that under wraps until we've seen the Baxters,' Alice replied and Brad nodded his agreement.

'Not yet, Mr. Vassel,' McCall growled, removing his hand. 'And don't worry, I'll see that P.R. let you personally know as soon as we've anything new.' Banging down the receiver, he returned to the squadroom. 'It's time P.R.

handled calls like that instead of feeding them to us. Do those shiny-butts downstairs reckon we're running a news service on the side?'

Before Alice or Rafferty could think up a suitable reply, Brad hung up.

'No answer,' he said and looked towards the doors. 'What's this, Tommy. You started mind-reading?'

'Humble Oriental detective see honourable lady fuzz and respected partner from locker-room door. Make number-one kind smart deduction that will need more than three cups of coffee. Brought extra for you.'

Crossing the room while speaking, Deputy Chu set down his loaded tray on his team's desk. However another man followed him into the room. A big, burly man who, despite wearing a well-cut business suit, managed to give the impression he was on his way to a duck-blind for a morning's pass-shooting.

'Do I smell coffee?' asked Lieutenant Jed Cornelius of the Firearms Investigation Laboratory.

'It looks like Oriental fuzz's deductive powers have gone back on him,' Alice remarked, without counting the number of cups on the tray.

'Humble self deduced that some excellent gentleman would smell aroma of coffee,' Chu stated, sounding like a Chinese detective in a 'B' movie. 'So bring *three* extra cups.'

'Deuced clever, these Chinese,' Brad said admiringly.

'How's the case going, Alice?' Cornelius inquired, taking one of the cups.

'We've made the victim as Fairy Manders, a girl wrestler—'

'Huh!' Cornelius sniffed. 'I don't think they should let women wrestle.'

'I don't see why not,' Alice replied. 'Unless it bruises the male ego to see women invading men's territory.'

'The Firearms Registry haven't come through with our list yet, Alice,' Brad put in before the subject of female equality could be enlarged upon. 'We're trying to trace all the British .38s in the county, Jed.'

'I'll goose them along in the morning,' Cornelius promised.

'Reckon it'll be worth doing, Brad?' Rafferty inquired.

'G.I.s brought in plenty of guns from World War II and Korea that were never registered.'

'Not so many,' Cornelius objected. 'Not British guns, anyways. The British army was a whole lot tighter than ours where guns were concerned.'

'Anyways, a gun brought in like that could have changed hands a dozen times,' Chu went on. 'Why don't you run a check on pawnshops for recent sales?'

'That would mean calling on the local houses for help,' Alice pointed out.

'They'll love you if you do,' McCall admitted, for the town's police divisions would have to assign detectives to the check of the pawn-shops.

'You could be wasting your time, and theirs,' Cornelius warned. 'I've been working all day on the bullets we dug out of the body. From the powder residue on them, I'd say they were loaded more recently than World War II or Korea. The bullets are standard British War Department issue.'

'So the guy bought them from a limey soldier over there,' Rafferty suggested.

'Could be,' Cornelius agreed. 'I've been reading up on the British .38/200 service cartridge. It was declared obsolete in March 1958. Of course the guns were phased out gradually. A dealer over here bought several batches when they became available. Which doesn't help, as he sold them to several companies.'

While Cornelius spoke, Brad stood with a thoughtful frown on his face. At last the big blond set down his cup and looked at the firearms expert. 'Do you have copies of this and last month's *Guns & Ammo* on file, Jed?'

'Sure, why?'

'I'm not sure, but I think I saw something in an ad. about British revolvers.'

'I'll go fetch them,' Cornelius offered, leaving the room.

While waiting for the firearms expert to return, McCall told Alice and Brad that Jack Tragg and the district attorney were holding a conference to decide what action should be taken against Flaker. Cornelius' return, carrying two firearms magazines, interrupted Rafferty's blunt, if not altogether practical, views on how to deal with the hippie.

'Here it is,' Brad said, after turning the pages of the September issue and halting at a full-page advertisement. 'Special bargain, bonus offer by Turner & Grail, New York. An Enfield Number Two, Mark One .38 service revolver and an official British War Department box of eighteen bullets, price fifteen dollars.'

'Anybody who bought one would have the right kind of bullets,' Alice admitted. 'We'd best contact Turner & Grail and ask if they sold any of their bargain offers to Rockabye County, or even Texas addresses.'

'I've already contacted them,' Cornelius put in. 'Not about the bargain offer, but asking about sales of British revolvers in general. There are only half-a-dozen major distributors handling British war surplus firearms and I've wired them all. With luck, you should have replies tomorrow or Saturday. Then all you have to do is bring me the gun and I'll match up its bullets.'

'What I like about you, Jed,' McCall said dryly, 'is the way you always keep the hard bits for yourself.'

'I was born that way,' grinned the firearms expert, retrieving his magazines. 'See you around.'

Alice dialled the Baxters' number as Cornelius left, but nobody answered.

'You'd best run up there in the morning,' McCall suggested.

'Shall we take SO 12?' Alice asked.

'Nope. Go up in one of you's car. I'll give you a chit to fill its tank at the official pumps.'

'We'll take my M.G. then, Alice,' Brad grinned. 'Unless you're going to pull rank on me.'

'The M.G. will do,' Alice replied.

'You may as well log off now and make an early start,' McCall informed them. 'I'll call you if anything develops.'

At the municipal employees' parking lot, Brad reminded Alice of the promise she had made after the meeting with the hooker, Mabel. Never a girl to go back on her word, Alice invited Brad to her apartment and kept the promise.

CHAPTER TEN

'THERE's nothing like a refreshing day in the wide-open spaces, boss-lady,' Brad commented, sounding like a travel bureau salesman, as he swung his imported M.G. MGB convertible from Route 118 on to the Morgan Turn-Off at nine-thirty on Friday morning. 'Especially when it's at the tax-payers' expense.'

'Sure,' Alice replied, settling comfortably in her seat and touching the safety-belt around her. 'Did you get this so your girl-friends can't escape?'

'How you do talk woman,' Brad grinned. 'I never once had one try to escape on me. You for sure didn't last night.'

Since risking their lives together, acting as decoys to bring the murderous Colismides' gang into the open, Alice and Brad had become very close. They took in movies when off watch, or spent the evenings – and on occasion the whole night – together at his or her apartment.

Forgetting the case for the night, Alice and Brad managed to relax without interruption. They had visited the Sheriff's Office to see if there were any new developments, before starting out to visit Fairy Manders' trainers. Finding nothing, they had filled the M.G.'s tank at the official petrol pumps and set off for Calverton. The town lay beyond the county line and the Morgan Turn Off offered the most direct route to it.

Passing the place where the body had been discovered drove all the levity from the deputies.

'Do you think Jack's right in not holding Flaker for trial?' Alice asked.

'Sure,' Brad replied. 'It saves us time in court. And if we'd done it, the anti-gun tabloids would've made him a martyr. I reckon the d.a. and Jack called it right, leaving him in the wino-tank* until morning, then turning him loose.'

* Wino-tank: Cell used for chronic alcoholics and bums.

'He was in choice company,' Alice smiled. 'Whew, the smell.'

'The drunks and bums had to put up with it,' Brad replied. 'He was a touch loud, come to—'

'Brad!' Alice put in. 'I think that grey Ford sedan's tailing us.'

'Do, huh?' Brad answered, glancing in the rear-view mirror. 'Want me to stop?'

'No. Not yet, anyways. In the woods here he could run by and when we caught him claim he thought we planned a stick-up. Anyways, I'm not sure he is after us. There was a grey Ford parked in front of the Public Safety Building, but I didn't get its number.'

'Best take it now,' Brad suggested. 'There should be a set of field glasses back of the seats.'

Tapping the quick-release clip, Alice freed the safety-belt. Then she twisted around, picking up the cased field-glasses from among the fishing tackle behind the seat. With the convertible's hood up, she could study the following vehicle and avoid being detected. However the Ford lay some seventy-five yards behind them and the dust stirred up by the M.G. did not aid vision.

'I've got the number,' Alice said, turning around and nodding to the Voice Commander radio. 'We'll see what he does at Morgan's Corners. If he's still after us, I'll call Cen-Con and ask them to have D.M.V. make the owner.'

'Know the driver?' Brad asked.

'I can't make enough out. He's got a beard, longish hair and is wearing sunglasses. Can you leave him behind?'

'If I can't, I've wasted money buying this imported heap,' Brad grinned.

Building up speed, Brad soon left the Ford behind. They caught glimpses of it as the road wound through the hilly country, for it did not turn along any of the side tracks leading to farms or hunting cabins. However, once they went through Morgan's Corners, they saw no sign of the car and concluded that it had been behind them by chance.

In that they guessed wrong.

The killer had been out front of the D.P.S. Building, meaning to try to learn if the law was any further advanced with its investigations. Seeing Brad and Alice arrive, then turn to the rear of the building instead of into the municipal employees' parking lot, he awaited developments. Normally private vehicles were not allowed in the official parking area unless they were to be used on official business, for which petrol was supplied. Wondering what the business might be, he decided to trail them when they left.

On seeing the M.G. swing on to the Morgan Turn-Off, he first thought that the deputies intended to take another look at the scene of the crime. Only that did not call for the use of a private car. They would use an official vehicle when conducting a routine investigation within the county.

Within the county!

Calverton lay outside the county line and could best be reached by following the Morgan Turn-Off.

Fairy Manders had told the killer about the Baxters' training camp for girl wrestlers. Indirectly that had been the cause of her death. But the deputies did not, could not, know of the Baxters.

Unless they had identified the body!

There had been no mention of it in either the local newspapers that morning. In fact the case received little attention due to news of an American space-shot filling the public's interest.* Of course, the police and sheriff did not give all they knew to the press. They might be withholding the fact that they knew the victim's name.

A cold sweat crept over the killer. Maybe the deputies were closer to him than he imagined. Yet he could see no way in which they might connect him with the dead girl.

At which point he became aware of how close he was to the M.G. So he slowed the Ford and watched the little convertible fade away. He knew how to find the Baxter place. So he decided to allow the deputies a good head start, drive there and see if that was their destination.

All through the drive to Calverton, the killer tried to tell himself he had no cause for concern. However he continued to keep the car rolling until he saw a signboard pointing along a track through wooded country and read the

* The space-shot gave the *Lightning* an excuse to ignore Flaker; they did not wish to make a martyr of him. Probably the *Mirror* saw no way of presenting their part in the affair satisfactorily, for they also made no mention of the false confession.

78

name 'T. Baxter' on it. Stopping the car off the road, he went down the track on foot. As he started to turn a corner, he saw a building ahead. Moving more cautiously, he came into sight of a small modern ranch house, with a large barn and other buildings. Not that the layout of the place interested him. His main attention focused on the M.G. convertible standing before the house.

The deputies *had* identified Fairy Manders.

Then he saw Alice and Brad come from the house accompanied by a couple he decided would be the Baxters. Turning, he ran back to his car. As he drove in the direction of Calverton, he kept a watch on the road behind. However he went through the town and reached the Morgan Turn-Off without seeing the deputies.

Fear and anger filled him as he drove along the Turn-Off. Those damned deputies knew too much. He wondered if he should leave town. Doing so meant giving up a well-paid job which he would be unable to duplicate in another town. If there was only some way in which he could throw the deputies off his trail—

A track, its entrance hidden by bushes, flashed by, the ground on the other side of the road falling off in a steep, rock and tree covered slope. Almost without thinking, the killer stopped his car. He sat looking around him for nearly a minute, thinking furiously. An idea formed, one which might not entirely solve his problem but ought to delay the investigation. Every day he gained increased his chances of safety. Time blurred the memory. The longer the law took to find anybody who had seen him with Fairy Manders, the smaller grew their chances of getting someone who remembered it.

With that in mind, he backed the Ford into the mouth of the trail. Climbing out, he walked along the Turn-Off and made sure the car was out of sight. Then he returned to find a place from which he could watch the road without being seen. He felt that he could hardly have chosen better. Higher up and almost a mile away, a stretch of open country gave him a clear view of the road. There would be time to return to his car and make all ready when he saw the M.G. cross the open section.

Any car going over the edge of the road and down the

79

slope would seriously injure, or more probably kill, its occupants. Of course the deputies would have passed on all their findings in the case to their superiors, but the investigation was sure to be delayed. Even if the Sheriff's Office did not think Fayde and Counter were killed in an accident, its deputies would follow the usual routine of looking for criminals with a grudge against the dead officers. That would further delay the Manders' investigation.

The killer did not have long to wait. Seeing the M.G. he turned and ran back to the Ford. With a hand that shook a little, he turned the ignition key. Filled with a mixture of fear and excitement, he made all ready to charge out when his victims went by. Counter was driving at a good speed. When he saw the Ford rushing at him, he would swing away hurriedly and either drive or be knocked over the grass verge on to the slope.

CHAPTER ELEVEN

AFTER paying a courtesy call to the Presidio County sheriff's sub-office in Calverton, Alice and Brad went on to the Baxter place. Nobody was in sight as they climbed out of the M.G. Hearing thuds, gasps and squeals from the barn, they went to investigate.

On entering, they found themselves in a well-equipped gymnasium. Half a dozen good-looking girls were working out on various pieces of equipment around the room. In its centre was a full-sized wrestling ring where a couple of attractive girls, a red head and a brunette, were putting on a fast paced bout. A small woman wearing stretch pants and a sleeveless sweater supervised the girls. Despite being older and plumper than on the photograph in Connie Storm's office, the deputies recognized her as Bubsy Baxter.

'Not that way, Mona!' the woman yelled as the brunette flipped over the redhead's shoulder and landed hard. 'Break the falls with your hands and feet, not with your veins. Go into the wind-up, Red.'

'Mrs. Baxter?' Alice said, walking forward.

'The woman turned. 'Sure. Hold it up a minute, will you? The kids are just going into their wind-up.'

Leaping forward as Mona rose, Red attacked. For a time Mona seemed to take the worst of it, with Red bouncing her around the ring. Then, as the redhead rocked off the ropes in a shoulder charge, Mona side-stepped. Linking her fingers, she drove her interlocked hands into Red's shoulders. Shooting across the ring, the redhead struck the turnbuckle in a corner with some force. She flopped back on to her rump and remained sitting, shaking her head dazedly from side to side, until the count reached eight. As Red rose groggily, Mona darted forward. The brunette caught Red around the knees, tumbling her on to her back, and sank down to bend her double. Sitting on Red's thighs, Mona held her immobile while Busby counted her out by a pinfall.

'O.K., kids,' Bubsy said, rising. 'That's fine.'

Crossing the ring, the woman ducked between the ropes and dropped to the floor. Behind her, the girls stood up, sweating, breathing hard, but apparently none the worse for their strenuous work-out. Busby looked first at Brad, then gave Alice a long scrutiny.

'You're not in bad shape,' Bubsy remarked. 'Let me feel at your biceps.'

'Go ahead, Alice,' Brad said with a challenging grin.

Flexing her arms, Alice allowed the women to press at her biceps.

'Not bad,' Busby said. 'Have you done any grappling?'

'Not in a ring,' Alice admitted.

'It's a tough life,' the woman warned. 'And it's only the top twenty or so girls who earn enough for mink coats and Cadillacs.'

'We're not wrestlers, Mrs. Baxter,' Alice replied and took out her id. wallet. 'We're deputies from Rockabye County.'

'If some night-spot's been putting on topless wrestling bouts, or somebody's making girl-fight movies, none of my kids are involved!' Bubsy stated indignantly.

'It's not that, Mrs. Baxter,' Brad told her.

'What can I do for you, then?' Bubsy asked. 'Come up to the house, we can talk better there. Red, Mona, go take a shower. The rest of you kids carry on exercising until I get back.' Then, as she accompanied the deputies from the gym, she went on, 'You pair would make good wrestlers. You've got the shape for it, Miss—'

'Fayde,' Alice said.

'Does it have to be formal?'

'Alice Fayde. This is my partner, Brad Counter.'

'Pleased to meet you,' the woman said. 'Call me "Bubsy". If I ever had another name, I've forgotten it. Sorry I jumped you like that, but there are so many creeps and bluenoses always looking for some way to knock girl wrestling. I don't get it. They can put filth like "Hair" on the stage, or any anti-American trash in a movie and get praised, while the same folk who do the praising treat girl-grappling like dirt and try to get it banned.'

'I always figure critics are the editor's idiot kin who he has to employ but can't trust with any useful work,' Brad remarked. 'You should maybe have all your girls shouting "End American imperialist aggression in Vietnam" at the start of every bout. Then you'd get good reviews.'

'I'd sooner go out of business,' Bubsy grinned. 'What brought you here?'

Before the question could be answered, they reached the house. A tall, grey-haired man, still powerfully-built although he walked with a limp, came around the side of the building. Bubsy introduced him as her husband, Tom, and escorted the deputies into the sitting-room.

'We've come about one of your girls, Fairy Manders,' Brad said.

The Baxters exchanged glances, then looked at Alice and Brad. Baxter hitched up his jeans and said, 'What about Fairy?'

'Where is she?'

'She was supposed to be in St. Louis last night,' Baxter replied. 'It was the start of a three month circuit. But she didn't show. Do you know where she is?'

'She's not in any trouble with the law, is she?' Bubsy went on and there was genuine concern in her voice.

'No, ma'am,' Brad answered quietly.

'We think she's been murdered,' Alice went on.

Letting out a gasp, Bubsy sank into a chair. Tom Baxter sucked in his breath and stared at the deputies. There was no mistaking that the news came as a complete shock to the couple. Not even professional actors could have simulated it.

'Dead!' Baxter repeated. 'When? How?'

'She was murdered on Monday,' Alice explained. 'We found the body early yesterday morning and didn't tell the press we'd identified her.'

'We tried to reach you on the telephone yesterday,' Brad continued. 'Couldn't get a reply.'

'There was nobody here after two in the afternoon,' Baxter said slowly. 'We took the girls over to Euclid Air Base to put on a card for the air crews. It's a regular thing, the fly-boys like it and it gives the girls a chance to work out before spectators.'

'Was she the woman on the Morgan Turn-Off?' Bubsy breathed.

'Yes,' Brad admitted.

'But the papers and newscasts said— How did you—?'

'She had on a leopard skin bikini and we traced it to Connie Storm,' Alice replied. 'She told us about you and we asked her not to call you.'

'Don't sound so surprised,' Baxter said. 'If Connie promised not to, she'd keep her word.'

'We have to ask questions,' Brad warned.

'Go to it,' Bubsy snapped. 'Anything to nail the bastard who killed her.'

'When did you last see Fairy?' Alice asked.

'On Sunday. She drove out to check on the circuit,' Bubsy replied.

'She wasn't staying here then?'

'No. We wanted her around Gusher City to be handy for visiting the doctor. You knew she'd been out of the game with a knee injury?'

'We heard,' Alice replied. 'It was one of the things which helped identify her. Where did she stay in town?'

'At the apartment we keep for girls who appear in Gusher City. It's in our apartment building, 91 West Street.'

'Do you know if she had any friends in town?' Alice inquired.

'She never mentioned any when she came out here,' Bubsy replied. 'I reckon she had though, Fairy was a nice guy and got on with folks.'

'Unless they started knocking girl wrestling that is,' Tom Baxter put in. 'It was one subject she felt strongly about. Say, can we offer you a drink and a bite to eat?'

'Just coffee, thanks,' Alice smiled.

'And a meal, unless you ate on the way here,' Bubsy insisted. 'Tom handles a mean skillet.'

'Then we'll stop and eat, thanks,' Alice accepted. 'Did Fairy mention having any boy-friends, Bubsy?'

'Not to us,' the woman replied and her husband nodded agreement before leaving the room. 'Say, though. Bill Muldoon might know. He's the super at the apartment building and knew Fairy.'

'We'll see him on the way home, Brad,' Alice decided. 'So Fairy never brought anybody out here with her?'

'No. She knows we don't like too many folks knowing about the training camp. Not that we're ashamed of what we're doing, but it attracts weirdos we can do without. The bluenoses knock us enough without giving them openings.'

'Did she have any enemies among the other girls?' Brad inquired.

'She had feuds, but nothing serious,' Bubsy replied.

'And none of her opponents hated her?'

'Not enough to kill her, Alice. Why should they? A well-publicized feud's good business. It gets the ring-worms interested and boosts attendances. No, even if two girl wrestlers hated each other, there'd be no killing. It pays too well having the other girl around.'

'You can't think why anybody would want to kill her?' Brad asked.

'None at all,' Bubsy admitted. 'Aren't you going to ask me where Tom and I were on Monday?'

'We'd have got round to it,' Alice smiled. 'Not that there's any need.'

'Thanks,' Bubsy said and meant it. 'Anyways, Monday is the evening we have the Allardyces over for bridge.' She smiled, 'Do you know Sam Allardyce?'

'He wasn't at the office when we dropped in on the way through Calverton,' Brad admitted. 'But we know him.'

'He shoots the Mexican Defence Course real good,' Alice went on, grinning at her partner.

'He's just lucky,' Brad protested, for Deputy Sheriff Sam Allardyce had narrowly beaten him during a shooting match some time before and the opportunity for revenge had not yet come.

'He's the same way at bridge,' Bubsy chuckled, on learning the reason for Alice's comment. 'It took us until four in the morning to get the last rubber our way.'

Although Alice and Brad questioned the trainees, none of them could offer any clue. Fairy had helped with their training, been well-liked, but did not discuss her private life. After a good lunch, Alice and Brad walked out of the house with the Baxters. They stood on the porch for a time talking, then the deputies climbed into the M.G.

'I'm strapping myself in,' Alice stated, adjusting the seat-belt. 'After eating all that Southern-fried chicken, you're likely to fall asleep at the wheel.'

'Come over some time and we'll show you some movies of our bouts,' Busby offered as Brad also fastened his seat-belt.

'We'll do that,' Alice promised.

By the time they reached the road, the killer's car was out of sight. Calling at the Calverton sub-office, they found that Deputy Sheriff Allardyce had returned and he confirmed the Baxters' alibi. Not that Alice and Brad disbelieved the couple, but their training demanded that they checked.

Wanting to reach Gusher City and resume their investigation, Brad drove at a fast pace along the Morgan Turn-Off. Satisfied that the Baxters knew nothing about Fairy Manders' death, they decided to visit the apartment house in passing and before reporting to the Sheriff's Office.

'I'll try to raise Cen-Con and tell them,' Alice remarked, picking up the Voice Commander radio, as they sped along a section of road lined with thick bushes at the left side and a steep slope beyond the grass verge to the right.

Drawing out the radio's telescoping aerial, she extended it over her left shoulder and through the open window. Even as she glanced at the aerial, Alice heard the rising growl of another car's engine. The mouth of a track flashed into view and she saw the grey Ford shooting from it.

'Brad!' she yelled.

Already attracted by the sound of the Ford's engine, Brad was looking to the left. At the sight of the car leaping in their direction, his driver's instinct caused a subconscious and potentially dangerous reaction. Ramming down his foot on the brake, he started to swing the M.G. sharply to the right. Instantly he saw the danger and set about averting it.

To continue in his present direction would see them mount the grass verge and plunge down the slope. Not even the seat-belts could save them from serious injury or death if that happened. So his powerful right hand spun the steering wheel around and his left flashed down to apply the brake. Responding like the thoroughbred it was, the M.G. obeyed the dictates of the controls. In turning, its right front wheel struck the hard ridge caused by the road wearing below the level of the grass verge. With an audible plop the tyre burst, but the M.G. was already skidding to a stop.

Everything happened so fast that Alice had little time to think. Looking to the left, she saw the Ford loom closer, then flash by. Its driver had planned to side-swipe them rather than go for a head-on collision which might also damage his car and leave him with no means of escape. By pure luck he had timed his move almost perfectly. Only Brad's superb reflexes and the M.G.'s excellent handling qualities had prevented the attempt from being a success. Slammed forward by the convertible's sudden change of pace and direction, Alice lost her hold on the radio and it flew from her hands to crash into the dashboard. The seat belt snapped tight around her, preventing her from pitching after the radio.

'The crazy son of a bi—' Brad began as the M.G. stopped, watching the Ford career away, weaving across the road as its driver fought to regain control.

'It's that grey Ford!' Alice interrupted, reaching for the quick-release fastener of the seat-belt. 'I'll—'

The words died away as she stared at the radio. Hurled against the dashboard, it lay between her feet with its front crushed in.

'If I hadn't been wearing that safety-strap—!' Alice breathed.

'Yeah!' Brad agreed, freeing himself and opening his door. The Colt automatic swivelled into his hand as he landed on the grass verge. Running along the road, he reached the corner around which the Ford had disappeared but could see no sign of it. Turning, he holstered his gun. 'He's kept going, Alice.'

'I figured he might,' she replied. 'Can we get after him?'

'Not until I've changed tyres.'

'Damn it! And the radio's bust. He'll get clean away.'

'Did you see him?' Brad asked.

'Only vaguely,' Alice admitted. 'I couldn't pick him out on a line-up.'

'It was that grey Ford that followed us, though,' Brad stated. 'We've got his number, he can't know that. I'll change the tyre, boss-lady, then we'll ask D.M.V. who he is and go pay him a little call.'

'I'm looking forward to that!' Alice said grimly.

CHAPTER TWELVE

WHILE Brad worked on changing the tyres, Alice examined the side track and surrounding bushes. She found where the killer had hidden to watch for their coming and hung a handkerchief on a near-by bush to act as guide for the S.I.B. experts when they arrived to search for footprints and other evidence.

'We'll have them out here, Brad,' she remarked, rejoining her partner. 'It was a try at us.'

'Yep,' Brad agreed. 'You'd best drive the rest of the way, boss-lady. If he tries again, I'll see what a couple of .45 bullets'll do to change his mind.'

Raising no objections, Alice slipped behind the M.G.'s steering wheel. She shot 'Expert' on the County's exacting qualification course, but knew Brad to be far better.

The need for Brad's gun-skill did not arise, for they saw no sign of the grey Ford. Stopping at the first gas-station on Route 118, Alice identified them as deputies and asked the owner to let Brad use the telephone. On dialling the Department of Motor Vehicles and requesting a make on the Ford, Brad was surprised at the reaction of the man taking the call.

'This isn't for another parking ticket, is it?' came the reply in an indignant growl.

'I don't get it,' Brad said.

'I did. Last night at half past six. I'd been kept late checking some licence numbers of Auto-Theft and was just going home when a call came in asking for a make on that damned Ford. And what is it, but some rookie harness bull'd seen a hippie jump a parking meter down on Baines Avenue. He'd called in himself, with—'

Listening to the words, Brad remembered that he had picked up Alice on Baines Avenue the previous evening at around half past six. He also recalled her description of the Ford's driver, so interrupted the D.M.V. man's story.

'Where was the parking meter on Baines?'

'How the hell should I know,' growled the voice at the other end of the line. 'I'm only the poor sap who goes around checking the records.'

'I bleed for you,' Brad told the speaker sympathetically. 'Who owns the car?'

'The Tonto U-Drive Hire Service. "U" as in the letter, not in "you". They're on Sutton Road that's in Evans Hill.'

'Thanks. I was going to call Traffic and have them check their street maps for it.'

'That wouldn't surprise *me*,' replied the D.M.V. man and hung up.

Grinning a little, Brad checked on the list printed on the cover of his notebook and dialled the number of the Leander Division station house. Patrolmen from that division handled Baines Avenue. The desk sergeant who took Brad's call sounded even less amiable than the man at D.M.V.

'If this's another rib—' he began menacingly.

'It isn't. Where did your man see the Ford?'

There was a pause while the sergeant checked the blotter,* then he replied, 'Meter 1851. Out front of the Perma-Curl Beautician Parlour. Say, was Shatzer on to something?'

'Could be,' Brad admitted. 'We'll be around to see him later.'

'I'll keep him around the house then,' the sergeant promised.

Hanging up the receiver, Brad rejoined Alice and told her what he had learned. The girl nodded soberly, right hand going to the flap of her bag.

'We'll have to forget the apartment house,' she said. 'Let's get to the office and tell Mac about this.'

'I didn't bother calling in for a general on the Ford,' Brad remarked as they returned to the M.G. 'It's only hired, so he'll likely dump it as soon as he gets into town.'

'It's likely,' Alice agreed. 'He's probably dumped it already. Let's go.'

On arrival at the squadroom, they reported to the watch

* Blotter: Official log of incidents and arrests.

commander. As they expected, McCall treated the near-wrecking of the M.G. as a murder attempt.

'He must have tailed me when I went to see my informer yesterday,' Alice said. 'Then followed us this morning. And when he lost us, took a chance on our coming back along the Turn-Off.'

'Then we'd best see if anybody using the Turn-Off—' Brad began.

'I'll put Larsen and Valenca on it,' McCall interrupted.

That was standard procedure. A peace officer going out to face down the bad guy might have worked in the days of the old West, but a modern law enforcement department did not operate that way. Sure Alice and Brad wanted to get the would-be killer, but that very desire might cloud their judgment. So they would leave finding the Ford's driver to Deputies Larsen and Valenca, continuing their own investigation.

Calling the two deputies – Larsen a giant of a man with a soft, gentle voice and Valenca of slender, medium height – into his office, McCall gave them the case. Neither showed any surprise that they had been assigned to it. Returning to the squadroom with Alice and Brad, they set to work.

A murder attempt on a peace officer mostly stemmed from revenge. So, while Larsen called the Tonto U-Drive Hire Service, Valenca asked the routine questions. Although they discussed a number of people who might want Alice dead, none of the deputies connected it with the Manders' case. Larsen learned that the Ford had not been returned to its owners and asked to be informed if it should be. As the clerk who hired the car out had already gone home, Larsen obtained her address. Alice could not provide a description of the driver, but the clerk or Patrolman Shatzer might be of more assistance.

'Where're you two going?' Valenca asked, after calling R. and I. to obtain details of Alice and Brad's cases from which suspects might be found.

'Over to West Street,' Alice replied.

'We'll tag along and see if he follows you,' Larsen suggested. 'Use your heap, Brad, so he'll know it.'

'Sure,' Brad agreed. 'It's across in the municipal employees' parking lot.'

'Give us time to get into an undercover car then,' Larsen said.

During the drive across town to West Street, Alice kept a watch on their rear. They arrived without being followed, other than by Larsen and Valenca in an unmarked car.

'Want us to stake you out while you're inside?' Larsen asked.

'I don't think you'll need to,' Alice answered.

'We'll go see the harness bull and the clerk then,' Valenca decided. 'Watch how you go.'

91 West Street was a large, modern-looking three-storey building in a middle-rent district. Leaving the M.G. parked at the sidewalk, Alice and Brad went inside. Alice knocked on a door marked 'Superintendent' and a big, heavily-built old man with a broken nose and cauliflower ear came out.

'Tom Baxter sent us,' Alice announced, holding out her id. wallet and the note Baxter had given her at the farm.

'Badges, huh?' the man rumbled. 'Tom and Bubsy ain't in no trouble, are they?'

'Should they be?' Brad asked.

'Listen, feller,' the superintendent answered, low and menacing. 'Tom and Bubsy're good folk. They treat all their gals right, get 'em the best deal they can. And they fit me up here after I got bust up and couldn't wrestle no more.'

'They're in no trouble,' Alice assured the man. 'They're helping us. We'd like to see the apartment they keep for the girls who're in town.'

'That's what the letter says,' the man admitted. 'Come in and I'll let you have a key. There's nobody using it now.'

'How about Fairy Manders?' Brad asked, following Alice and the man into a neatly-kept apartment.

'Fairy? She left on Tuesday for a circuit down South. Fairy's big on the Southern States circuit.'

'Did you see her leave?' Alice asked.

'Naw! She saw me Monday afternoon and said she was going Tuesday. I was out most of Tuesday and I ain't seen her around, so I figu— Hey! What's with the questions? Is Fairy in trouble?'

'She's dead, Mr. Muldoon,' Alice said quietly, watching the man's face and seeing it register shock.

'Dead!' Muldoon muttered. 'How'd she die?'

'She was murdered,' Alice told him.

'Who by?'

'That's what we're trying to find out,' Brad answered.

'Yeah!' Muldoon growled, prowling the room like a winter-starved bear hunting for food or fight. 'Well when you get him, whoever did it, leave me have him for a spell.'

'You liked her then,' Brad said as Muldoon stopped pacing.

'Everybody in the building liked her,' the man replied. 'She'd drop in here for a cup of coffee, or to watch the grappling on the television. I was a meat-heaver, Wild Bill Muldoon they called me.'

'I saw you fight a couple of times,' Brad admitted. 'Did Fairy have any friends, Mr. Muldoon?'

'Why don't I go check the room while you talk to Mr. Muldoon, Brad?' Alice suggested.

'Be as well,' Brad agreed.

Selecting a key from a number hanging on a board, Muldoon handed it to Alice. Then, as she left the room, he turned to Brad.

'Like I said, everybody here was her friend.'

'Did she go around with anybody, a boy-friend maybe?'

'Not from here. There're middle-aged families or older in the other apartments. Fairy knew most of them, but nothing more.'

'And she never brought a boy-friend, or anybody back here?'

'Not as I know of,' Muldoon replied. 'I don't keep tabs on the roomers.'

'Did she go out much?' Brad asked.

'Sure, most nights. Hell, she was young and good-looking. And when she was on a circuit she never had time to get around.'

'Why not?'

'That gal took her work seriously and kept in training. When she was on a circuit, travelling and training didn't leave her with time to play around.'

'Do you have a gun, Mr. Muldoon?' Brad said softly.

A puzzled frown came to Muldoon's face, then anger twisted at it. For a moment Brad thought that the old man meant to attack him. At last Muldoon gave a low sigh and shrugged.

'You have to ask,' he said. 'Sure I've got a gun. It's registered.'

'What type of gun is it?'

'A Colt Woodsman. Do you want to see it?'

'It won't be necessary,' Brad replied, knowing that the gun in question fired .22 Long Rifle cartridges and would not handle a .38 bullet. 'I have to know where you were on Monday night.'

'Here,' Muldoon replied. 'The Carters, they live along the hall, came over. Their television set had broken and they came in, stayed to see the late-late show.'

'Thanks,' Brad said, walking towards the door. 'Like you said, we have to ask, Mr. Muldoon.'

Leaving the super's room, Brad visited the Carters. They confirmed Muldoon's alibi, but added nothing to Brad's knowledge of Fairy Manders. Before going to join Alice, Brad decided to talk with more of the ground floor roomers. At the third attempt he had a reward for his persistence. The occupant, a plump, cheery woman, had seen Fairy going out on Monday evening and remembered how the girl had been dressed. Writing down what the woman told him, Brad thanked her. As he left the apartment, a woman he had spoken to earlier came into the passage.

'Hey!' she said, looking in Brad's direction. 'There's somebody in Fairy's apartment. It sounds like they're throwing the furniture around.'

Without waiting to hear more, Brad ran along the passage and bounded up the stairs.

CHAPTER THIRTEEN

DONNING a pair of light cotton gloves, Alice unlocked the door of Fairy Manders' apartment and entered. She knew better than go in bare-handed and leave her fingerprints to cause extra work for the Latent Prints crew who would be called in. Leaving the door unlocked, so that Brad could enter when he arrived, Alice looked around. The apartment consisted of a large combined living and bedroom, a minute kitchen and small bathroom. It was clean, neat and would be ideal for accommodating a girl on vacation and so did not wish to spend too much time cooking or doing household chores.

Apart from a thin coating of dust there was nothing on the small table at the right side of the room, or the two chairs which stood with their seats tucked under it. The bed was made, a shortie nightdress on it. Crossing the room, Alice placed her shoulder bag on the sidepiece at the left by the kitchen door and opened the wardrobe next to it. A dress and coat hung inside, with a couple of large suitcases on the floor. Both the cases weighed heavy enough to be full, so Alice carried the top one to the bed after testing the catches to see if she could open it. On raising the case's lid, she found it held Fairy's ring outfits; two pairs of monogrammed ring boots, a couple of white swimsuits, a black sweater and ballet tights, much patched and darned, that she probably used for training and finally a diaphanous white robe which Fairy wore when walking to or from the ring, and half a dozen towels.

The second case held the girl's street clothes, but yielded nothing to help find her killer. Returning it to the wardrobe, Alice closed the door and went to the sidepiece. She drew open the top drawer and looked in. It held a handbag which she removed and opened.

94

Hearing the apartment's door open as she reached into Fairy's handbag, Alice thought Brad had arrived. So she looked over her shoulder and opened her mouth too comment on the result of the search. What she saw made her turn and stab her hand towards the Pete Ludwig bag.

Coming into the room, a brunette woman tossed her coat aside and kicked the door closed behind her. She was Alice's height, a few years older and maybe ten to fifteen pounds heavier. Wearing a metallic-looking sheath dress, the newcomer had a figure that would hold its own in any company that did not have Connie Storm's 'skeleton fetish'. Her hair was done in a bubble cut and her attractive face had an expression of anger on it as she moved towards Alice.

Instead of entering the bag, Alice's hand caught and knocked it from the sidepiece. Of all the peace officer's equipment in the bag, it had to be the Colt Commander that slid into view. Instinctively Alice bent down, meaning to collect the Colt and return it to its holster. She almost made it.

After glancing at the gun, the brunette sprang forward to dig her left hand into Alice's hair and heave upwards. Alice felt as if the top of her head was being torn away as she was hauled erect. Coming round, the brunette's right hand slapped hard across Alice's cheek. The slap spun her around so that she landed upon her back on the bed.

While it was not the first time Alice had been slapped by a woman, she could not remember taking one which carried so much weight behind it.

Quickly the brunette thrust Alice's bag and gun under the sidepiece. Then she kicked off her shoes and flung herself towards the bed. Seeing the woman coming, Alice raised her legs. The brunette landed on Alice's feet, her weight bending the redhead's legs. Alice felt her knees burst through the nylon stockings and a suspender strap broke. Then she exerted her strength to straighten her legs and heave the brunette back across the room. Even as Alice pushed, the brunette's right fist flailed around and caught her nose in a painful manner.

Going back across the room, the brunette hit a wall and rebounded from it. Alice bounced off the bed, too angry to think of anything but repaying the slap and blow to her nose.

Up and out shot her fist, thrown as she had been taught at the G.C.P.D.'s academy. When the punch landed, Alice figured it ought to flatten that over-stuffed brunette like a wet flapjack.

Only the punch did not land. Before the fist reached her face, the brunette brought up both hands to catch Alice's wrist. Carrying the trapped wrist upwards, the brunette pivoted under it. Alice's feet left the carpet and she felt herself somersaulting over. Just in time she remembered her self-defence training and broke her fall.

Releasing Alice's wrist, the brunette dug fingers into her hair. Once again she hauled Alice erect and heaved the girl across the room. Unable to halt her forward rush, Alice managed to get her hands up to prevent being crashed face-first into the wall. Hearing the brunette's feet pattering towards her, she turned. Out lashed Alice's right arm, her hand open and held for the *tegatana*, hand-sword, blow of karate. Its edge slashed into the brunette's neck, halting her. Following it up, Alice drove her left fist into the other woman's belly. It was a good punch, with a power that had on previous occasions ended the objections of a hooker, booster or female drunk to being arrested. Taken in such a manner, the other women had gone down in a gasping, winded heap and caused no more fuss. Although the brunette gasped and withdrew a couple of steps, she kept on her feet.

For a moment the girls stood glaring at each other. Alice ought to have used the respite to inform the brunette of her peace officer's status, but did not. Even as the thought came, the brunette lunged at her with hands reaching to take hold.

Instinctively Alice snapped out a punch. Her knuckles cracked crisply against the brunette's chin, jolting the head back without stopping the advance. Throwing her other fist, Alice saw the woman weave aside. Then the brunette was behind her. Whipping her right arm over the red head, the brunette hooked it across Alice's throat and gripped the left shoulder of the bolero jacket.

'Lousy – little – crud!' the brunette hissed, maintaining her strangle-hold and punctuating the words by driving her left fist into the deputy's back.

Except for Joan Hilton, Alice had never come up against

such a strong woman; and her experiences with Joan had been during training sessions in a gym. The punches only travelled a few inches but they landed hard enough to hurt.

Desperately Alice grabbed at and tried to pull the arm from her throat. She could not and almost panicked. Then her training gave the answer. Curving her body forward, she slammed her buttocks back into the stomach behind her. Letting out a gasp, the brunette loosened her hold. Catching the arm, Alice hauled it from her windpipe and used it as a lever to throw the woman over her shoulder. Alice ought to have read the danger in the way the woman broke her fall and lessened the impact of her arrival on the floor. Instead she started to follow the brunette down. Raising her legs, the woman thrust them up over her body. The soles of the feet caught Alice under the breasts. Agony tore through her, she cried out in pain and reeled back against the kitchen door.

Bouncing off, Alice saw the brunette regain her feet with a bound. They came at each other, with Alice gaining a judo *tai-otoshi* body drop. However the brunette not only broke her fall expertly, but brought Alice somersaulting over as she landed.

For a time they churned over and over in a purely feminine tangle, with hair pulling, legs and arms flailing, teeth closing on flesh. During the wild mill Alice felt more suspender straps break and the stocking slid down around her ankle; its mate laddered and lost a knee. She wriggled out of the bolero jacket and her blouse parted company with the denim skirt, dragging open at the front under the brunette's hands. Not designed for strenuous activity, the brunette's dress burst at its seams.

They rolled the width of the room twice in their wild tangle. Then Alice gained a momentary advantage, straddling the brunette's recumbent body by kneeling between the spread-apart legs and bending forward to clamp both hands about the other's throat. Raising the woman's head, Alice slammed it against the floor. Although the mat absorbed most of the impact, Alice figured more of the treatment ought to cool the brunette down.

Before Alice could repeat the blow, she felt the brunette's legs lock around her body. Crossing her ankles, the

97

brunette started to apply a crushing pressure. Her knees ground into Alice's sides below the rib cage. Pain caused Alice to release the brunette's throat. Rearing back, she tried to force the legs apart. The muscles under her fingers felt like steel, she could make no impression on them. Clearly the brunette knew how to make the most of a scissor hold. She tightened her grip in a series of jerks which brought tears to Alice's eyes.

Croaking with pain, Alice reared up. Then she slammed her clenched fists into the brunette's bust. Crying in agony, the woman opened her legs. She lashed up a punch which tumbled Alice from her. The force of the blow rolled the deputy across the floor until she was halted by the bed. Using it to haul herself upwards, she saw the brunette also rising. Pain twisted the woman's face as her hands went to her bust. For all that, she advanced towards the bed.

'The dress flapped loosely, showing the brunette's figure. Exhausted and hurt as she was, Alice understood what she saw. Although built on generous lines, with what was once called an hour-glass figure, the woman wore only a bra, nylon panties and a garter-belt connected to her ruined stockings. Alice realized that to retain such a slender waist without artificial aids, the woman must be exceptionally fit.

Exceptionally fit. Just like Fairy Manders. And the brunette had entered the room as if she possessed every right to do so.

'Oh Lord!' Alice thought, as the brunette dropped into a wrestler's crouch and came forward. 'I've tangled with a girl grappler!'

Absurdly, considering the danger, Alice recalled her stand in McCall's office on women's right to become wrestlers if they wished. With her body throbbing in pain, she hurriedly revised her opinion. Not only should women be barred from wrestling, she decided, but the ban ought to have been imposed the day before the brunette started to learn.

Swooping forward, the brunette caught Alice's tangled red mop and started to drag her erect. Putting off her opinions, Alice gave thought to protecting herself. She knew that she had made a mistake when the brunette entered; but doubted if the woman would stand and listen to explanations right then. Equally exhausted and aching, she was too angry to be reasoned with. So Alice did not try. Instead she clenched her right fist and slammed it hard into the brunette's lower belly. Gagging in agony, the woman released Alice's hair and staggered away bending nearly double. Almost falling herself, Alice linked her fingers, hooked her hands under the brunette's chin and heaved. Thrown backwards, the brunette started to go down. Following her, Alice saw her break her fall on her hands; standing on her palms and feet with her body arching in a wrestler's bridge. Then the brunette thrust herself upright, ducked her head and lunged to butt Alice in the midsection.

Breath burst from Alice's lungs as she reeled under the impact. The brunette grabbed Alice by the waist and stumbled after her. Going down, Alice acted on pure reflex. She managed to get a foot against the brunette's stomach and shoved with it as she hit the floor. Thrown upwards by Alice's leg and her own impetus, the brunette's buttocks struck the wall. Her body came down on to Alice's and lay draped across the deputy's.

For a time they stayed like that, too exhausted to move. At last Alice weakly tried to roll the brunette from her. The feeble effort jolted the brunette into motion. Slowly she dragged herself into a kneeling position, one hand on Alice's bust, the other knotting into a fist.

Bounding up the stairs well in advance of the woman, Brad saw two suitcases and handbag outside Fairy Manders' apartment. He could hear nothing from the room as he went forward. Drawing his automatic, he kicked open the door and went in fast.

While expecting trouble, the sight which met his eyes brought him to an amazed halt. Staring at the two girls, Brad realized that he must do something. Pressing the Colt's safety-catch, he dropped the automatic into his jacket pocket and closed the door. Then he crossed to where the brunette was drawing back her fist for a blow at the weakly struggling Alice. Gripping the woman under the arms, Brad lifted and heaved her across the room. She let out a gasping squeal, landing belly down on the bed.

Much as Brad wanted to see to Alice, he attended to the brunette first. Any woman who could tangle with Alice Fayde and come so close to beating her must be tough. So Brad felt disinclined to take chances. Taking out his handcuffs as he went to the bed, he secured the brunette's wrists behind her back.

'Is everything all right in there?' called a querulous voice from the passage.

Not wishing to have witnesses before he knew what had happened, Brad crossed the room and stepped through the door without letting the woman beyond it see inside. He decided that the woman, having told him of the disturbance, had a right to an explanation and invented one.

'It's all right, ma'am,' he said. 'My partner's just met one of her old college buddies and their sorority greeting's a mite rowdy.'

It said much for the trust and respect Jack Tragg had built up around the Sheriff's Office that the woman accepted Brad's explanation. However she merely gave a sniff which indicated nothing college graduates did would surprise her and replied:

'Ask them to hold it down a bit, will you?'

'Sure will, ma'am,' Brad promised, picking up the cases and handbag. 'They said for me to tell you they're sorry you've been disturbed.'

Back in the room, Brad found Alice sitting against the wall. Mouthing muffled curses, the brunette wriggled off the bed. In doing so, she exposed most of herself to the big blond's eyes. However Brad did no more than take one good look before turning to Alice.

'How do you feel?' he asked, gently helping her to rise.

'I wish I was dead!' Alice gasped as Brad led her to the table, drew out a chair and sat her in it. 'Has she blacked my eye?'

'Nope,' Brad replied, studying her face. 'Forget the female vanity. What the hell's come off here?'

For a moment Alice did not reply. Then she touched her jaw and groaned, 'I think I goofed.'

At which point the brunette twisted round, tugging against the handcuffs. Then she realized what the cold steel about her wrists meant and glared at Brad, trying to rise.

'You dumb cop!' she screeched. 'I live here when I'm in town. She's the one!'

'Like I said!' Alice breathed. 'I goofed.'

'Lemme loose!' the brunette yelped. 'I'll soon make her tell the truth.'

'What happened?' Brad asked, looking from Alice to the brunette.

'I came in and caught her going through Fairy Manders' handbag and she tried to pull a gun on me is what!' the brunette answered.

'Who are you, ma'am?'

'Helen Whitsall's the name. I work for the owners. Why in hell aren't you asking her the questions?'

'I know the answers,' Brad replied. 'She's Woman Deputy Alice Fayde. Shield number W401—'

'A deputy,' Helen spat out. 'What kind of malarkey's this—?'

'Turn her loose and let me show her my badge, Brad,' Alice said, rising and limping across to the sidepiece. 'Then you'd best go out of here until we've made ourselves presentable.'

After seeing Alice's id. wallet, Helen Whitsall accepted Alice's *bona fides* but showed indignation. However Alice started to smooth things over after Brad left to continue questioning the other roomers.

'I'm sorry for what happened, Miss Whitsall,' she said. 'If I'd found a stranger searching a friend's property, I'd have done the same.'

'Yeah,' Helen answered. 'When I saw that gun—'

'I wasn't trying to draw it,' Alice interrupted. 'I only wanted to show you my id. wallet.'

'Hey!' Helen ejaculated. 'What're you doing here anyways?'

'Fairy Manders was murdered on Monday,' Alice replied bluntly.

'Murd—!' Helen gasped. 'I'm sorry, she was a damned nice kid.'

'How well did you know her?'

'We've done circuits together. I was the bad guy and Fairy the goodie.'

'Do you mind if I go on asking questions?' Alice said, rubbing her side.

'I can take it if you can,' Helen answered, touching her bloody nose.

'Did you get on together?' Alice asked, accepting the unspoken challenge.

'She was a good guy,' Helen replied. 'And I mean outside the ring. You know something, she could out-wrestle me any time. But she insisted that we took turns to win.'

'I'll fix your nose,' Alice offered.

'Let's call it a draw and both fix ourselves, huh?' Helen grinned and held out a hand. 'No hard feelings?'

'Not if you haven't,' Alice replied, shaking hands.

Half an hour later, dressed in one of Helen's blouses and a pair of the brunette's stockings, Alice felt in condition to resume the questioning. While patching up the fight damage she had learned that Helen was in town for a wrestling match on Monday. The brunette had come to the apartment house, meaning to stay there over the week-end. Having a date that evening, she had come straight up without calling in on Muldoon, so did not learn of the peace officers' presence in the building. Entering the apartment and finding Alice searching it, she drew the wrong conclusion.

Sitting at the table, with cups of coffee before them, Alice asked, 'Was Fairy a dyke?'

Anger glowed in Helen's eyes and she hissed, 'How'd you like to try another fall?'

'Simmer down,' Alice said quietly. 'I have to ask them no matter how they sound. Fairy went around with a bull-dyke for some time. I'm not saying you're one.'

'Sure, Alice. It's— Well, like I said, Fairy was a good guy and, as far as I know, she wasn't a dyke. We've double-dated when we've been on a circuit, with meat-heavers who've been on the card with us mostly. I don't see a dyke doing that.'

'Did she go steady with any of them?'

'Not steady, or serious. Fairy wouldn't let anything come between her and wrestling. She made enough at it to pay for an operation her mother needed and to keep the old lady in a high-price sanatorium. Being able to do that meant a lot to her.'

'Can you think of anybody who would want Fairy dead?'

'Not in the grappling game,' Helen replied. 'She got on good with folks, in and out the ring. There was only one thing got her riled, if somebody started knocking girl wrestling. She got us arrested in New England one time for tossing a joker who'd been giving us the knock over the bar in a night-spot.'

'Did she have a temper?'

'Only if somebody riled her by cracking wise about wrestling. She took grappling real serious.'

On his return from questioning the other roomers, Brad found Alice and Helen on surprisingly good terms considering how they first met.

'There're three families I haven't seen,' he told his partner. 'They're not at home. Two women saw Fairy going out on Monday at around seven thirty. She was dressed in a cloak-coat and blue mini. One of the women saw her getting into a cab across the street, couldn't hear where she said to go and doesn't know which company the cab was from.'

'We ought to be able to trace it,' Alice guessed. 'Her bags are packed. I'd say she intended to make the circuit, she's got all her ring kit, Helen tells me.'

While waiting for Brad, Alice had completed her search and asked Helen's opinion on what she found.

'Anything in the bags?' Brad asked.

'Only her bank pass-book and a cheque book,' Alice replied. 'There're no unusual withdrawals, or large ones recently. Nothing to show she might have been blackmailed and was killed when she got tired of paying.'

'That's another motive gone,' Brad said. 'What now, boss-lady?'

'I'm going to call in a lab crew,' Alice replied. 'We may as well see if they can find traces of visitors. Then we'll go back to the office. Thanks again for helping us, Helen. I'll let you have the blouse and stockings back.'

'Sure, Alice,' Helen replied with a grin. 'I want you in the ring sometime – with a referee. You fight dirty.'

'So do you,' Alice smiled back, touching her arm where Helen's teeth had left a bruise.

Helen showed them to the door, the robe she wore over her underclothing parting enough to give Brad a view of what lay beneath. 'Come around any time – both of you.'

'I wouldn't have it any other way,' Alice assured her.

'That's a nice gal,' Brad commented as he and Alice went downstairs.

'Yes,' she agreed coldly, adjusting the bag on her left shoulder.

'So're you,' Brad went on. 'And I like you best, even if you did get licked.'

'Licked!' Alice gasped. 'Why you—'

'Come on,' Brad interrupted. 'I'll let you buy me a meal before we report back in.'

'And they say the days of chivalry are dead,' Alice sighed. 'I'll buy the meal – again. But don't let me catch you sneaking back here alone.'

CHAPTER FOURTEEN

CLAIMING that paying for it gave her the right to select where they had their meal, Alice directed Brad to the Badge Diner. Owned by a policeman retired through a wound gained when the county had its big clean-up, the Badge stood a block away from the D.P.S. Building and attracted much trade from the local peace officers.

While eating, the deputies were joined by two detectives from the Narcotics Detail. The conversation turned to their work and the detectives told how what they hoped would be a promising tip from an informer had turned to nothing.

'We thought we had him,' Sergeant Simpson, big, burly and pleasant-looking, said. 'It was Al Rimmer, used to work with Tippy Hale, Alice. You remember him?'

'Sure,' she agreed.

'Harry and me picked up a whisper that Rimmer had two pounds of h. and was set to pass it along,' Simpson went on, nodding to his equally big and burly partner. Sergeant Harry Gotz had a broken nose and a long scar ran down his left cheek, giving him a rough, brutal expression. 'We went round to ask him about it. What do we see but Rimmer leaving his pad with a package in his hand. So we tail him, figuring to put the arm on whoever he's delivering to. We trailed him to one of the long-hair joints in Green Valley. As we went in, there was Rimmer handing the package to his gal. They opened it up for us—'

'And?' Brad prompted.

'It was full of candy,' Gotz finished.

If detectives from any other squad had made such a confession, the deputies would have ribbed them. There was nothing amusing about narcotics and the possible distribution of two pounds of heroin did not strike Alice and Brad as the subject for jokes.

'What then?' Alice asked.

'Rimmer insisted that we went back to his pad and searched it,' Gotz replied.

'We went and looked,' Simpson continued. 'Nothing.'

'So the pigeon was wrong,' Alice said, knowing the men to be very thorough and capable of finding the heroin if it had been concealed in Rimmer's apartment.

'Maybe,' Simpson answered. 'Only Rimmer stopped at a mail box. We could see the package in his right hand all the time, but his left hand was out of sight. He could have had the h. ready for mailing, hidden under his coat, and dropped it in without us catching on.'

'Trouble being the box'd been emptied time we got around to figuring that,' Gotz went on miserably. 'No chance of finding what was in it. All we can do now is put stake-outs to watch Rimmer and his known associates for a few days and hope one of them gets the package.'

'I hope you nail him,' Alice said and Brad echoed the sentiment.

With the meal over, Brad and Alice returned to the Sheriff's office. There McCall told them of Larsen and Valenca's findings. The car had not yet been returned to the company which owned it.

'We've an A.P.B. out for it,' the first deputy went on. 'Lars and Tony called in. The car was hired by a James B. Passingham, of 12 George Street – only he isn't. Folks who live there've never heard of him.'

'Didn't the company that owns the heap check him out?' Brad demanded

'Nope. He produced a valid driver's licence, a business card and the cash for the hire, that's all they needed. The car's insured,' McCall replied. ' "Passingham's" a tall, slim cuss, dressed like a hippie. The harness bull gave a description, I've put a copy of it on your desk.'

'And the rest of this stuff,' Alice said, indicating the pile of papers in the 'In' tray.

'Aye,' McCall agreed. 'You'll likely be wanting to read through them.'

'Lucky Mac didn't ask how I spent the afternoon,' Alice smiled as the first deputy walked back into his office.

'Nothing shows you've been fighting,' Brad assured her.

'It may not show,' Alice sighed. 'But I sure as hell know I have.'

Taking up the first of the papers, Brad looked at it. 'Great Western Arms in L.A. say they haven't sold any English revolvers hereabouts. Got a negative from Klein's in Chicago, too.'

'I.C.R. can't make Fairy Manders from her prints,' Alice commented, reading another report. 'That means she's clean in Texas.'

'*No!*' Brad said in surprise, for he knew I.C.R. received details, including fingerprints, of every person arrested in Texas and acted as a storehouse for such information.

'I never could stand a smart-alec partner,' Alice sniffed. 'No kick-back from the F.B.I. yet.'

'Got us a list from the Firearms Registry,' Brad remarked and counted the names on it. 'Nine owners, only three in Gusher City. The sub-offices'll be able to check the others out. Reckon I ought to run over to West Street and see how the lab boys're getting along?'

'No I do not!' Alice stated. 'Anyways, Helen's got a date with Bronco Ed Gable tonight, so she told me.'

'In which case, I'm true to you, boss-lady,' Brad grinned, knowing the man to be a wrestler. 'I'll start calling the cab companies instead.'

'Go to it,' Alice replied, picking up another sheet of paper. 'S.I.B. have analysed that vomit. Steak, French-fried onions, boiled potatoes and apple turn-over, they make it. There's the necropsy report here and that's about all.'

Working methodically, Brad called the town's cab companies, asking each to check its records for a driver who had picked up a good-looking, shapely blonde woman at around seven-thirty, Monday evening, on West Street.

'What say we go see some of these gun owners while we're waiting for the answer,' he suggested.

'Sure,' Alice replied. 'We've lost our tail, but we'll take SO 12 in case he's around.'

'Be best,' Brad agreed.

'How about unregistered guns?' Alice inquired as she initialled the various reports prior to filing them with the other material of the case. 'Do any of the Rockabye County Combat Shooting Club have English revolvers?'

Brad looked both pained and indignant at the thought. 'We only let members use .38 *Specials* because so many peace officers have to carry that calibre. .38/200 and .38 Smith & Wesson definitely are out. Some of the cowboys who go for blank-popping at the Fast Draw club might use one though.'

There was a difference between the serious sport of combat shooting and the game of fast draw. In the latter only one thing counted, speed of draw and discharge; firing a gun loaded with blank cartridges or wax bullets as fast as possible without worrying about where the barrel pointed when the bang sounded. The problem posed in combat shooting as, 'How quickly can you draw, shoot and hit a target at various distances and under as near combat conditions as can be arranged?'

Serious combat shooters had little but contempt for blank-poppers. Brad's tone implied that anybody stupid enough to play that game might also be dumb enough to own an under-powered British revolver.

'We'll look in on them when they hold their next meeting,' Alice promised.

'If you say so, boss-lady,' Brad answered with no great show of enthusiasm. 'I can always wear a false beard so nobody'll recognize me. If any of the Combat Club see me going in there, they might think I've lost my marbles.'

Alice gave a gurgle of delight as she saw what a weapon Brad had put into her hands. In future, when he misbehaved, she would insist that they visited the Fast Draw club.

'Let's go see the gun owners,' she said.

'Brad!' McCall said, coming to the door. 'That was Jack calling. He wants you to give a shooting display for a couple of English policemen. They'll be here at four tomorrow.'

'I reckon I can,' Brad agreed, for he earned sixteen dollars a week extra on his pay by virtue of his shooting ability. 'What's Jack want me to do?'

'Just some fast draw and combat work downstairs,' the watch commander answered. 'Are you pair going out?'

'We thought we'd check on the owners of English revolvers

around town,' Alice replied. 'R. and I. haven't come up with any crooks who use them.'

'Watch your backs,' McCall warned. 'That jasper from the Turn-Off might make another try at you.'

Although Alice kept watch while Brad drove Unit SO 12 through the streets, nobody followed them. They visited each of the addresses on the list, asking questions and signing receipts to take in the revolvers for F.I.L. to run comparison tests against the bullets taken from Fairy Manders' body. It was uneventful, unexciting work that would probably prove unproductive, yet had to be done.

Shortly after leaving the last address, they received a call from Central Control. The Rockabye Cab Company had telephoned to say that one of their vehicles had picked up a blonde in West Street at around seven-thirty on Monday. Visiting the company's offices, the deputies questioned the driver. He identified Fairy from her picture – one of a number produced for Brad and Alice by Sam Hellman from the full-page photograph in *Ring Wrestling* – expressed his surprise at her employment, but gave little information. After collecting the girl, he had taken her to the front of the Rialto Cinema on The Street. Nobody had met her as she left the cab, nor had she entered the cinema when he drove away.

Yet even that little information helped. Slowly the detectives were tracing Fairy Manders' movements on the fatal Monday evening. Crossing town to The Street, they left the Oldsmobile in the Rialto parking lot. After visiting the cinema and failing to find anybody who could remember seeing Fairy, they started to visit the bars and cafés in the area. At each they asked their questions and left pictures of the girl to be shown to members of the staff not present.

Shortly before midnight Alice and Brad returned to the Sheriff's Office. They had not visited every place around The Street where Fairy Manders might have eaten with her killer, but planned to continue their search the following afternoon.

There was still the attempt on their lives to be remembered. Larsen and Valenca had been visiting people who might want the deputies attacked, but without results. The would-be killer could easily learn Alice's and Brad's home addresses from the telephone directory, so might be waiting for another try.

'Shall we stake you both out?' Larsen inquired.

'You can put one on Alice's place,' Brad replied. 'But she won't be there. We've talked it over and she'll be staying with me until this's over.'

CHAPTER FIFTEEN

'How's the case, Brad?' Vassel of the *Mirror* asked as the big blond deputy entered the basement pistol range at four o'clock on Saturday afternoon.

Already the cameras from the local television network were in place, the visiting English policemen, an inspector and sergeant, standing talking with Jack Tragg. Newspapermen, members of the D.P.S. Public Relations Bureau and other people milled around. Brad eyed the reporter up and down indifferently. Apart from wearing a white shirt, Vassel looked little different from on their last meeting.

'Which case, *Mr*. Vassel?' Brad asked.

'The Turn-Off murder. You and Alice Fayde have it, don't you?'

'Do we?'

'So play cagey,' Vassel said. 'That could mean you're not doing so well and haven't even identified her yet.'

'How's Mrs. Greer?' Brad inquired pointedly.

A dull red flush mounted on the reporter's sallow cheeks and he turned to walk away. It had been while conducting a clandestine affair with Mrs. Greer that he first met the team of Alice Fayde and Bradford Counter.

Brad's dislike for what the reporter represented did not account for his reticence. For one thing Vassel could obtain details of the case from P.R. Another reason was that Alice had said they would keep the victim's identity under wraps. No matter what went on between them during off watch hours, Woman Deputy Alice Fayde was senior member of the team when on duty and what she said went. Until Alice gave him the go-ahead, Brad had no intention of divulging information about the case to reporters.

Coming across to where Brad stood, a member of P.R. and the television producer told him what they wanted. He admitted it would be easy enough to do as they asked – P.R. knew enough about combat shooting to arrange a spectacular display – and went to make his preparations.

First he emptied the powerful combat-loaded rounds from his magazines and replaced them with ordinary factory-charged bullets. He did not aim to waste his duty ammunition target-popping when D.P.S. bullets would serve as well. With the magazines re-charged and Colt holstered, he went to the firing line and turned to face the spectators.

Seven yards behind where Brad stood, five man-sized and-shaped silhouette targets stood against the back-stop. In the centre of each target's chest was a ten inch balloon.

Putting aside all thoughts of Vassel, even though the reporter was standing among the onlookers, Brad listened to Jack describing how gun-fighting techniques had changed since the days of his Great-grandpappy Mark.

'Except when he's in uniform, the jet-age deputy doesn't walk around showing he's packing a gun,' Jack went on. 'Which doesn't mean he's slower with it than in the days when Dusty Fog and Mark Counter ran the law in Mulrooney, Kansas. Take Deputy Counter there. He's on his watch and he hears something behind him—'

At the last word Brad pivoted around. In turning, his left hand unbuttoned the sports jacket and drew its flap aside. Working in smooth conjunction, the right hand rose, crossed and swivelled the automatic free from the holster's springs. Not until it slanted towards the first target did Brad allow his forefinger to enter the triggerguard and thumb down the enlarged stud of the manual safety catch. For all that, the instant he completed his turn, his automatic bellowed and the balloon on the right end target burst. Continuing to swing his gun, riding its recoil, usuing the waist high F.B.I. combat crouch and instinctive alignment, he burst the other four balloons in succession.

Not only the visiting policemen but the other onlookers showed their surprise. So well had Brad's tailor done his work that none of them had realized he was wearing a gun as big as the Government Model automatic under his jacket.

While the range staff made ready for the next display, Brad also made preparations. Going to the loading bench at the side of the room, he removed his jacket and stripped off the shoulder holster. Strapping on his official gunbelt, he placed the automatic – after changing its magazine for a fully-loaded spare – into its Bianchi-Cooper combat bikini. Steel-lined, forward raked, brief in size, the holster was one of the fastest ever designed and ideally suited to the techniques devised by combat masters like Jeff Cooper, Jack Weaver, Elden Carl or Thell Reed.

The range staff had brought out a 'balloon burst' target. This was a five foot high pole, with a wooden bar on a swivel at its top end. A ten inch balloon at each end of the bar balanced and held it horizontal. As Jack explained, when one of the balloons was burst, the weight of the other would tilt the bar.

Taking the .38 Special revolver offered to him, the British inspector joined Brad on the seven-yard firing line. Adopting the traditional target-shooter's stance, left arm at his side, profile on to the post, the inspector aimed. Brad stood with his gun holstered. On a blast from the British sergeant's police whistle, Brad speed-rocked the Colt from leather. Its detonation crack echoed the bark of the revolver and both balloons burst. The inspector's bullet struck just an instant ahead of Brad's but not enough to make the .45 bullet miss the sinking baloon.

For the next try at the 'balloon burst', the inspector had to start lifting his revolver into the aiming position on the signal. This time he stood no chance at all. When the whistle sounded, Brad's Colt left the holster and roared before the revolver could be raised and aimed. Exploding, Brad's balloon caused the bar to tip until it stood vertically in front of the supporting post.

Chuckling, the inspector declined to match himself further against Brad. So the big blond demonstrated other combat techniques. He worked from the holster, making hits at distances all the way back to the thirty yards line. If there had been more room available, he would have gone farther from the targets. For his finale, he stood before an electronic timing device. On a signal which started the timer, he drew, fired and planted a bullet into the X-ring at the centre of a silhouette target in one quarter of a second.

'I wouldn't have believed it was possible if I hadn't just seen it,' the inspector stated, when asked by a television interviewer what he thought of the way Brad handled a gun.

The comment came as no surprise to Brad. On various occasions he had seen combat-shooting experts perform feats, using heavy-calibre handguns and full-duty loaded bullets, which no television producer dare show his Western hero doing for fear of being accused of wild impossibility.

There had been the time when Sheriff Jack Weaver of Lancaster, California, drew his revolver and, using the double-handed hold he had perfected for long range shooting, burst a ten-inch balloon one hundred yards away with his first shot. Another of Weaver's feats had been to draw his *revolver*, fire at and hit twelve ten-inch gongs in succession at thirty yards, reloading half-way through the string, in *eight* seconds. Another combat master Elden Carl, had been matched against a shotgun expert to see who could be first to hit a ten-inch gong at fifteen yards. Carl started with his cocked automatic holstered and with the safety applied, the other man holding the shotgun down in front of him and at arms' length. On the signal to commence, Carl drew and fired four shots into the gong before the shotgun reached its user's shoulder and cut loose.

Brad could claim to be in the same class as Jack Weaver and Elden Carl, although the restrictions of the indoor range did not permit him to display his full dexterity.

After listening to the interviewing of the visitors, Brad turned to leave the range. In passing, he glanced at Vassel. The reporter was looking his way, but turned his head. Not, however, before Brad had noticed the worried expression on his face. Brad wondered if Vassel was recalling how he had argued instead of obeying the deputy's order to face the wall on the night he had been caught fleeing from the Greer house. Whatever his reasons, Vassel made no further attempt to ask questions about the Turn-Off killing.

On his arrival at the squadroom, Brad found it empty but for Alice and Valenca. They turned his way and Valenca grinned broadly.

'When're you going on the Ed Sullivan Show, Brad?' he asked.

'When he meets my price,' Brad replied. 'Have you

nailed this guy who tried to knock off the cream of the Office yet?'

'I thought we were after the feller who missed you pair,' Valenca answered. 'Anyways, we've got the car. A harness bull found it in a movie house parking lot in Green Valley.'

'This morning?' Brad asked.

'Around *one* this morning,' Larsen answered, coming from McCall's office. 'We went over there and had it hauled in. Latent Prints came up with a set. No make by R. and I., but we've sent a copy to I.C.R., maybe they'll make them.'

'Nobody's been tailing you today?' Valenca asked hopefully.

'No,' Alice answered. 'I went to the Turkish baths this morning for a massage and Brad tagged along behind.'

'Nobody,' Brad stated.

'We'll just have to keep looking,' Valenca sighed. 'I don't suppose any of your informers've picked up a whisper that there's a contract out on you?'

'If they have, they've kept it to themselves,' Alice replied. 'I don't see them doing that. Let's go, Brad.'

'Where to?' he asked.

'We'll take those three revolvers back to their owners. F.I.L.'s cleared them. Then we'll call in at 91 West Street and see the families we missed yesterday. After that, we'll hit the other places in The Street.'

Although they achieved the first two parts of Alice's plan, the last eluded them. S.I.B. had sent a team to Fairy Mander's apartment the previous evening, finding no fingerprints or other evidence that she had entertained anybody at it. None of the people the deputies questioned could add to their knowledge. So Brad drove the Oldsmobile in the direction of The Street.

'Cen-Con to Unit SO 12,' crackled the car's radio.

'SO 12 by,' Alice answered into the transmission microphone.

'You on to anything hot, Alice?' demanded McCall's raw tones.

'Nothing that can't wait,' she replied.

'Come in "Code Two", I need you. "Code One"?'

'Roger and out,' she replied, hanging the microphone on its hook.

There was no time for lengthy conversations, except in extreme necessity, over the radio. However McCall had told the deputies all they needed to know. 'Code Two' meant to treat the call to return as urgent but not to the extent of using red light and siren. When McCall had said 'Code One', he asked if Alice understood the message and her 'Roger' told him that she did.

McCall was alone in the squadroom when they returned.

'I wanted you on hand when Rafferty and Chu come in, Alice,' the watch commander said and held out an official message form. 'But this came in just now.'

'We've got a live one, Alice,' Brad commented, accepting and reading the message. 'Turner & Grail, New York, sold by post one Enfield Number Two, Mark One revolver, serial number 3935, eighteen rounds of .38/200 British service ammunition and, as an added bonus not mentioned in their ad., an instruction book put out by the British army for use of the gun. It came to a James M. Pallfret, 18 Rio Grande Street.'

'When?' Alice asked.

'Three weeks back,' Brad answered. 'Reckon we'd best go talk to Mr. Pallfret, don't you, boss-lady?'

'I reckon we h—' Alice began.

At that moment a considerable commotion sounded in the passage. The squadroom doors burst open and Deputy Rafferty brought in a prisoner. Hauled in might be a better word, for the Irishman was dragging the man by the links of the handcuffs coupling his wrists. The prisoner was almost as big as Rafferty, burly and with an unshaven face that looked like it had recently emerged from being used as a punchbag for a heavyweight boxer. Blood ran from a cut on Rafferty's cheek and his top lip was swollen. From all appearances, the man had committed the folly of resisting arrest. Tommy Chu followed his partner into the room, leading and supporting a thin, bruised-up woman wearing a torn dress.

'This's him, huh?' McCall growled, eyeing the prisoner coldly.

'This's him, the darlin',' Rafferty agreed and thrust the man into a chair. 'Sit there, darlin'. And if I was you I'd be keeping a civil tongue in me head. These folk here care less

116

for a wife-beating, baby-deserting son-of-a-bitch than I do.'

'I'll take Mrs. Goldberg into your office, Mac,' Tommy Chu remarked.

'I'll come and help you,' Alice went on, guessing that she had been recalled to attend to the woman.

Suddenly the prisoner lurched erect, swinging up his manacled wrists and lunging towards the woman. Rafferty caught the man's right arm, turned him and hit him in a manner that would have caused the deputy's instant disqualification had he been in a boxing ring. Agony twisted the coarse, brutal face. Clutching at his lower regions, the man collapsed to his knees.

'Don't do that sort of thing, darlin',' the burly deputy warned. 'Next time I might hurt you.'

'Take him upstairs, Pat,' McCall ordered. 'Go with him, Brad.'

'Yo!' Brad replied. 'How about this Pallfret *hombre*?'

'Tommy'll go with you,' the watch commander decided.

On the way to collect a car, after seeing the prisoner secured in a cell, Brad learned what had happened. One of Goldberg's neighbours had seen him leave his baby outside a five-and-dime, so called the police. Examination of the baby showed it had been starved and ill-treated. Sent to interview the parents, Rafferty and Chu arrived to find Goldberg beating up his wife for trying to report the baby's disappearance to the police. Already furious over the treatment of the baby, Rafferty showed Goldberg no mercy when the man attacked him.

'I thought Pat'd wind up in front of the County Commissioners' Disciplinary Board, way he handled that crud,' Chu finished. 'Only it seems that Goldberg was less liked than the law among the neighbours.'

'Knowing how Pat feels about kids, I'd say Goldberg came off lucky,' Brad stated. 'Do you know Rio Grande Street?'

'It was part of my beat when I was a patrolman.'

Taking Rafferty and Chu's car, the deputies drove across town. During the trip Brad explained their mission.

'Eighteen's a store of some kind,' Chu remarked. 'Wasn't Pallfret owned it when I walked the beat, but that doesn't mean much. He's still got the gun, hasn't he?'

'S.I.B. combed the area pretty good and never found it,' Brad replied.

Unconsciously Chu lowered his right elbow and pressed it against his jacket. Underneath lay his Smith & Wesson .41 Magnum revolver in a Myers Quick-Draw holster. The man they were going to interview had killed once and might resist arrest. However Chu knew he could ask for no better man at his side if they walked into a gun-fight.

Swinging the car along Rio Grande Street, Chu drove slowly, Number eighteen proved to be a seedy-looking second-hand store, its windows displaying a variety of articles. A sign reading 'CLOSED' hung in the darkened, glass-panelled door.

'How about it, Brad?' Chu asked, not stopping the car.

'The sign says Al Corram, not James M. Pallfret,' Brad replied. 'Let's check with the local house and see what they know about him.'

'I can take you to somebody a whole lot closer than the house,' Chu answered. 'And'll likely know more.'

'It's your range we're on,' Brad agreed.

Driving on, Chu turned a corner and halted before a small Chinese restaurant. 'Call in a "Code Seven"* and we'll put on the nose-bag.'

After telling Central Control that they would be off watch while having a meal, Brad followed Chu into the restaurant. A smiling waiter offered them a seat in the centre of the room, but Chu declined and went into one of the small alcoves. There he ordered water-chestnut soup, prawn curry and waffles in syrup as dessert.

A few seconds after the waiter left with the order, an older Chinese in a tuxedo came up carrying a tray on which stood two glasses of ice-cold beer. His teeth gleamed like a row of rifle butt-plates as he smiled at the deputies.

'Good evening, gentlemen,' he greeted, setting down the tray.

'Hi, Sam,' Chu answered. 'This's Deputy Brad Counter.'

Expressionless eyes flickered to Brad. The conversation was resumed in Chinese. Chu and Sam spoke fast, but quietly for a time then the man moved aside to make way for the waiter who brought the soup.

* Code Seven: Police radio code, off watch for a meal.

'Corram's a small-time grifter,' Chu remarked, picking up his soup spoon. 'He runs a postal accommodation address on the side.'

'You mean he rents out his address to folks who don't want their mail delivered to home?' Brad asked.

'Sure,' Chu agreed.

'I'll call him on the telephone and if he answers, we'll go see him,' Brad decided.

Brad paid for the meal and reimbursed Chu the sum given to the restaurant's owner for the information about Corram. Using the telephone in the owner's office, Brad tried to contact Corram but received no reply. So the deputies drove by the store, noticing that its upstairs rooms were also in darkness. Not wishing to warn Corram of their interest in him, they returned to the D.P.S. Building. McCall agreed with their actions in not knocking at Corram's door, saying Brad and Alice could try later.

When Alice returned from delivering the injured woman to the Central Receiving hospital, she and Brad went back to The Street. At last their persistence was rewarded. A waiter at a small grill on a side alley remembered seeing Fairy Manders on Monday evening.

'She come in around eight,' the man stated.

'Alone?' Alice asked.

'Naw, with a feller.'

'What did he look like?' Brad inquired.

'Tallish, not as tall as you though,' the waiter answered. 'Lean. He looked like a cleaned-up hippie. Long rusty coloured hair and beard, grey suit, psychedelic shirt, like that. Reason I noticed him was he didn't seem the kind of guy a swell-looker like the blonde'd have around with her.'

'Long rusty coloured hair, a beard and a psychedelic shirt,' Alice breathed. 'Brad, that could be the guy who was trailing us around.'

'Yeah,' Brad agreed. 'You'd best call in and tell Mac to pass the word about this to Lars and Valenca. They don't need to look for folks with a grudge, we know now who tried to kill us.'

CHAPTER SIXTEEN

SUNDAY mornings when on night watch were always a trying time for Alice since she and Brad had become so close. They invariably spent the night together, slept in late, indulged in a little love-making if the mood struck them and then Alice cooked breakfast while Brad read the Sunday supplement of the *Gusher City Mirror*.

In many ways Alice found amusement in watching the normally even-tempered Brad's reactions as he read the latest bigoted, intolerant liberal-intellectual sentiments. However experience had taught Alice it was better to avoid conversation during breakfast, then disappear into the kitchen and perform her chores until the smoke cleared.

'Vassel's at it again,' Brad growled, sitting at the table in his pyjamas.

'Huh huh,' Alice answered, setting down the plates. She had been up long enough to have taken a shower and wore only her bathrobe in the hope that the sight might distract her partner and allow them a peaceful meal.

'Listen to this,' the big blond went on. ' "I bought death through the mail".'

'He's on the anti-gun kick this week, huh?' Alice said.

'Yeah. Listen to it. "The mailman brought me the parcel. It looked innocuous until I removed the wrappings and opened the box. Inside it lay—" '

For a moment Alice thought sitting with her legs crossed and clear of the table had achieved its intention. Then she saw the change in Brad's expression as he continued to stare at the paper.

'What is it?' she asked.

' "Inside the box lay a revolver",' Brad read. ' "Its hexagonal barrel black and menacing, its cylinder ready to accept the brass-headed bullets from the packet of eighteen which lay by the gun's side. Under the revolver I found an instruction manual which told me how I could load and fire the weapon – how I could kill. I had bought death for only fifteen dollars—" '

'So?' Alice inquired.

'How many kinds of revolvers have hexagonal barrels?'

'I'm not sure,' Alice admitted, uncrossing her legs. If Brad had come on to something, there was no sense in distracting him.

Coming to his feet, Brad crossed the room. They had spent the night in his luxurious Upton Heights apartment – each kept a change of clothing at the other's place – so he had his library on hand. Taking a copy of Jeff Cooper's book, *Modern Handgunning,* from a shelf he turned its pages.

While Brad read the book, Alice studied the article in the *Mirror*.

'It can't be!' she gasped. 'There's no mention of the kind of gun.'

'There aren't many kinds with hexagonal barrels,' Brad pointed out. 'And even less that come as cheap as fifteen bucks.'

'Turner & Grail only sent one English revolver to Rocka-bye County,' Alice protested, although with little conviction in her voice. 'To James M. Pallfret—'

'Who uses an accommodation address,' Brad interrupted. 'You know how these intellectuals are. They're so egotistical that they figure they're one step better known than God. If he intended to buy a gun through the mail, Vassel'd reckon that Turner would say to Grail, "This's from the famous anti-gun bigot, Mr. Vassel of Gusher City, Texas," when they saw his order and not make the sale. So he'd use an assumed name.'

'He could have seen the ad. in *Guns & Ammo,*' Alice remarked.

'Which didn't mention the instruction book.'

'Or Palfret could have bought the gun and shown it to him.'

'Vassel's been nosing around, asking about our case mighty regular, boss-lady,' Brad reminded. 'But everything that's been in the *Mirror*'s come from Crossman.'

'So Vassel plans to write an exposé on our inefficiency.'

'Do you believe that?'

'We haven't a scrap of proof that Vassel even knew Fairy Manders existed.'

'And I don't like liberal intellectuals,' Brad said.

'Not even liberal-intellectuals like liberal-intellectuals,' Alice replied.

'Do we pick him up?' Brad asked.

'On what? That he wrote an article saying how he bought a gun.'

'He'd crack if we grilled him.'

'Before we could start, the *Mirror*'s legal department would have a lawyer at the Office sitting in our hip-pockets,' Alice stated. 'Let's wait and see what that feller from Rio Grande Street says about Pallfret first.'

'You're the boss,' Brad grinned.

'One thing you're forgetting,' Alice remarked, tossing the paper across the room on to the divan. 'The feller with Fairy on Monday evening had a beard— And the breakfast is getting cold.'

They ate in silence, yet each knew the other was thinking about the case. As Alice poured out coffee, Brad slapped a hand on the table.

'Did you see those false beards and wigs for sale in the store next door to Erotica Ltd., Alice?'

'Yes,' she admitted. 'For intellectuals who want to look hippie some of the time, but like human beings the rest.'

'That waiter at the Starlight Grill, he said the feller with Fairy looked like a cleaned-up hippie—'

'Tall, but not as tall as you and lean,' Alice quoted. 'Brad, how was Vassel dressed when he came up to ask Ric Alverez about our progress in the case?'

'A suit and—'

'A grey suit and psychedelic shirt,' Alice elaborated.

'Let's go nab him!' Brad snapped.

'I'm against it.' Alice replied. 'If he doesn't have the gun, we've no real proof. And if he did kill her like that, I want his hide. So I say we let it ride until we log on. Vassel's certain he's got us fooled, he'll not run for the border as long as he stays that way.'

'You want me to forget it?'

'I do.'

'Could try sitting with your legs crossed again,' Brad told her. 'The last time you did it, I near on forgot what day it is.'

'Did, huh?' Alice said, moving her chair back. Then she deliberately crossed her legs again.

Before leaving the apartment, Brad dialled Corram's number but had no reply. So he and Alice decided to visit Rio Grande Street on their way to the D.P.S. Building. Wishing to avoid warning Corram of the law's interest in him, they felt that going there in the M.G. would attract less attention. If he was absent, his neighbours would warn him on his return should the deputies arrive in an official car.

'It looks deserted,' Alice commented as Brad brought the M.G. to a halt across the street from Corram's store.

'Stay put, I'll check it out,' Brad answered.

A plump woman stood outside the vegetable store next door to Corram's place. A grin twisted her lips and she eyed the big blond in a knowing manner as he came over.

'Another of 'em, huh?' the woman greeted. 'Al won't be back until morning.'

'How's that?' Brad asked.

'G'wan!' the woman grinned and winked. 'You don't want your wife knowing the doll in the car writes you now and again.'

Then Brad got it. The woman took him for a potential client of the postal accommodation service. Her mistake was understandable. Especially on Sundays Brad dressed better than the average peace officer, few of which made calls in imported convertibles of expensive model.

Trying to act like a man caught out in something underhanded, Brad turned and walked back to the M.G. An idea began to form and he explained it to Alice as he drove them towards the D.P.S. Building.

Both Alice and McCall, when he heard it, agreed that Brad's notion was worth trying. The watch commander also sided Alice on the matter of moving warily when dealing with Vassel. Fear of the power of the press did not cause McCall's caution, but rather knowledge of the abuses papers like the *Mirror* put to their power.

Calling in a police artist, McCall requested his help in producing a sketch of the killer. Luckily the man knew Vassel, so created a perfect likeness to which he added long hair and a beard as described by Alice. When he finished, the girl held a reproduction of the man who had tried to run the M.G. off the road and who, she firmly believed, had killed Fairy Manders.

All that remained for the deputies to do was prove their suspicions.

CHAPTER SEVENTEEN

STANDING behind the counter of his store after putting the morning's mail delivery into a back room, Al Corram watched Brad Counter leave the M.G. and walk across the street. Nine-thirty on Monday morning was not a usual time for such visitations, but the storekeeper never looked a gift-horse or customer in the mouth. The girl in the car and the big blond's attitude as he approached the door told Corram that he had a client for his lucrative side-line. By the time Brad reached the counter, Corram had estimated the cost of his suit, shirt, country-club tie, shoes, wristwatch and the leather briefcase he carried.

Alice and Brad had spent a leisurely watch the previous night, in the squadroom cleaning the Office's assault armament and elaborating the plan he had formed due to the woman's reaction to their arrival outside Corram's store. Realizing that Corram would not co-operate willingly, they decided that Brad would arrive like a potential customer. So he dressed for the part and would have passed for a well-to-do young executive anywhere in town. Early in his career as a deputy, Brad had been on a stake-out covering a pornographic book-store. While awaiting the arrival of a young high-power who had killed two people in hold-ups, and who was known to spend much of his loot on pornography, Brad had been able to study the way law-abiding citizens acted when visiting the store. Putting his knowledge to good use, he had convinced Corram that he was coming to take an accommodation address but did not want anybody to know it.

'Howdy,' Brad greeted, setting the briefcase on the counter. 'Are you-all Mr. Corram?'

'That's me,' Corram agreed, glancing through the glass panel of the door at the M.G. and ignoring Brad's furtive manner.

'A friend of mine asked me to call in,' Brad said, after a couple of false starts and glances over his shoulder. 'He has some harmless correspondence that he doesn't want to go home—'

'So how can I help?'

'Well, I — my friend – he's got a friend, feller called James Pallfret, who allows you let him have a parcel sent here.'

For a moment Corram studied Brad's face. Everything about the big blond seemed right. That suit had been made for him, a feller with his build did not get such an excellent fit off a ready-to-wear rack in a store. He looked and spoke like a man high enough up the social ladder not to want mail from a girl-friend delivered to his home or place of business; especially if he had a wife. Such a guy would pay well for the use of an accommodation address and might also be open for a further bite as the price of Corram's silence about the transaction.

Yet he mentioned James Pallfret and did not strike Corram as being on friendly terms with the man who used that name. Of course, business exec's did sometimes go hippie, using wigs and false beards, on their own time.

Seeing the growing concern and impatience exhibited by Brad, Corram reached a decision.

'What name do you want the mail to come here in?' he asked.

'W. Smi—' Brad began. 'Hey! it's for my friend, not me!'

A mirror stood on the counter, placed so that a customer could see the door and street reflected in it. Hearing the door open, Brad glanced at the mirror. He saw a tall, well-built, quietly-dressed Negro coming in. Then, to his surprise, Brad noticed that Alice had left the M.G. and was crossing the street. More significantly, she was opening her handbag as she came.

Walking towards the counter, the Negro also looked into the mirror. He came to a halt, staring hard at the reflection of Alice opening the door.

'You lousy rat, Corram!' the Negro yelled. 'Cops!'

Then he swung round and sprang towards the door. Thumbing open the briefcase's securing catch, Brad turned to see the Negro lashing a fist in Alice's direction. The big blond's right hand entered the briefcase and emerged holding

126

his Colt automatic. While not sure what brought his partner to the store, Brad was ready to back her play.

Recognizing the Negro, Alice had guessed what might have brought him to Corram's store. So she crossed the street ready to take him. For once Alice made an error of judgment. Thinking that the Negro would not identify her, she started to enter the building. From his actions and words, he remembered her all too well.

Even as the fist drove towards her, Alice took a long stride to the rear and jerked the door closed behind her. Unable to stop it, the Negro drove his hand through the glass panel. It shattered and splintered, one pointed sliver ripping open his wrist and forearm. Alice twisted around, hunching her head forward, feeling flying glass patter against her back and hearing the Negro's cry of pain.

The sound of a door opening and closing stopped Brad as he moved to help his partner. Turning, he saw that Corram had departed and could only have gone through the door behind the counter. Swiftly Brad glanced over his shoulder, seeing the Negro's hand go through the glass panel. Given that brief respite, Brad figured Alice could handle the man. So he must get after Corram.

Dropping the briefcase, Brad vaulted the counter. He had not chanced wearing his shoulder-holster for the visit, knowing Corram would make him as a peace officer should the man notice the slight bulge it caused. Ducking his shoulder, Brad lunged forward and charged the door. Rio Grande Street was not the most stoutly built section of the city. So, while secured by a Yale lock, the door yielded to the impact of Brad's powerful body. Going through, he found himself in a poorly-lit dirty passage with several side doors and one at the end which probably was the store's rear entrance.

Thinking that Corram had bolted through the back door, Brad started along the passage. Then he heard the whirring of some kind of electric motor from a room to his right. Turning, Brad kicked open the room's door and entered fast with his automatic ready for use.

The room was a kitchen. However, a pigeon-holed rack on the wall held a number of letters and still more were on the table. Brad noticed the details, although Corram attracted his main attention. Standing by a whirring refuse-disposal unit at the sink, the man held a package.

'Hold it!' Brad snapped as Corram began to lift the package towards the open mouth of the unit. 'I'm a deputy sheriff. Drop that parcel.'

Looking back, Corram saw the way the big Colt lined on him and the set, grim determination shown by its user. Nothing about Brad led the man to assume he was making an idle threat. Perhaps Corram would have taken a chance against a peace officer armed with a snub-nosed .38 Special revolver. But there was something about the big .45 Government Model automatic which caused a man to think twice before making a wrong move.

'If the parcel goes in, you'll never walk again,' Brad warned, seeing the man's hesitation.

Corram gave a beaten shrug and turned. With the disposal unit still not working at full speed, he could not dispose of the package. Even if the lawman did not carry out his threat, there would still be evidence of the package's contents in the unit.

'Don't shoot,' Corram said.

'Bring it over here,' Brad ordered. 'Put it on this chair.'

Muttering sullenly, Corram obeyed. Brad's command had prevented him from placing the package on the table and later denying he had tried to destroy it. While crossing the room, Corram studied Brad. Not with the intention of jumping him. Corram's medium height and slim build did not lend itself to tangling with somebody Brad's size. Instead he studied the deputy's clothing once more. For a peace officer to be that well dressed, he must have an income over and beyond his salary. Corram knew of one source of income open to a lawman.

'Can't we be friendly over this?' he asked, putting the package on the chair and eyeing the big blond hopefully.

'Friendship's my middle name,' Brad answered.

'How much?' Corram said, and patted where his inside breast pocket would have been had he worn a jacket.

'Bribery?' Brad said.

'Naw!' Corram sniffed. 'Call it insurance.' Then he stared as Brad drew a pair of handcuffs from his left pants pocket. 'I can go as high as—'

'Save it until I see what cut my partner wants,' Brad told him.

'Yeah, but—'

'She cuts me in on all her graft,' Brad pointed out. 'What do you think I am, a double-crosser? Let's go see how she's making out.'

Alice was making out fine.

The sound of breaking glass attracted attention. Voices yelled and people began to converge on Corram's place. Ignoring them, Alice pushed open the door and went back into the store. After smashing the panel, pain from his badly-lacerated wrist had caused the Negro to stagger to the centre of the room. He stood facing the door, features twisted in lines of fury, the wrist gripped in his other hand and dripping blood to the floor. Despite that, he tensed ready to hurl himself at the girl.

'Don't try it, Tippy!' Alice warned, right hand coming from the Pete Ludwig shoulder-bag.

Staring at the gun she held, the Negro stood still. Instead of the snub-nosed revolver most women officers carried, Alice held a Colt Commander; smaller brother – by half an inch length and twelve ounces weight – to the big Government Model and with the same calibre. Tippy Hale did not even start to imagine that Alice drew the gun as a bluff, or lacked knowledge of how to use it. If she had to, Alice would shoot and send her bullets where she wanted them to go.

'You've got nothing on me!' the Negro muttered sullenly.

'Attempted assault for one thing,' Alice contradicted. 'Likely there'll be more if the parcel came.'

Having seen Brad vault the counter and follow Corram, Alice did not need to ask where he was going, or why. From her experience in the Narcotics Detail, she guessed what brought Hale to the store and hoped her partner had reached Corram in time to prevent the destruction of the evidence.

'If that rat Corram talked—!' Hale began.

'I'm not with Narcotics any more,' Alice interrupted. 'You just picked the wrong time to collect the parcel. I'll fix your arm when my partner comes back—Official business, folks, stay outside, please.'

While speaking, Alice had taken her id. wallet from the bag with her left hand. Without taking her eyes from the Negro, she held out the wallet for the first of the people attracted by the disturbance to see. Doing so prevented Hale from pretending that a hold-up was in progress and escaping in the confusion. If the store had been in Greevers, with its large Negro population, Hale might have called on the people to help him against the white peace officers. Unfortunately for him Rio Grande Street was in the Evans Park district; an area which at best only tolerated coloured people.

'What's he done?' demanded the woman who had first given Brad the idea for the deception.

'It's just routine,' Alice answered without turning. 'Have you a telephone?'

'Sure we have.'

'Would you call Central Control and ask for a prowl car, please? And bring me some bandages.'

Early in her career Alice had learned the best way to avoid questions was to find the person asking them something to do. Showing satisfaction at being requested to help, the woman not only left but shoved the other kibitzers out of the door and closed it behind her.

'Don't do me no favours,' Hale growled. 'If that bastard Corram talked, he'll wish he'd never been born.'

Before Alice could answer, a r.p. car halted outside. Its crew dismounted, pushed through the crowd and entered the store.

'Fayde, Sheriff's Office,' Alice announced, showing her id. 'That was fast.'

'Huh?' grunted the leading patrolman.

'I've only just sent to have a call put out,' Alice explained.

'We saw the crowd and came to take a look,' the patrolman told her. 'One time we didn't and there was a gal, real good-looker too, stripping off all her clothes. Feller don't want to chance missing something like that.'

'I'm sorry if I disappointed you,' Alice smiled. 'One of you fix his arm up, please, and the other go hold back the crowd.'

'Yes'm,' the patrolman replied.

Brad came from the door behind the counter, herding

Corram ahead of him. Watching the storekeeper, Alice saw him avoiding the Negro's eyes.

'Did you—' Alice asked, walking over to meet Brad.

'Sure did,' the big blond replied.

'Call Narcotics then,' the girl ordered, nodding with satisfaction. 'Tell them to send Simpson and Gotz to collect that package of "h".'

CHAPTER EIGHTEEN

AT no time during the half-hour they waited for the detectives to arrive did the deputies take Corram or the Negro out of sight of the crowd who hovered outside the store. Hale refused to answer any questions and sat nursing his bandaged arm. Intending to leave him in the hands of the Narcotics Detail men, Alice and Brad did not worry over his silence. Nor did they speak to Corram, who spent a worrying thirty minutes trying to decide how his action affected his future.

When Simpson and Gotz arrived, Brad escorted them into the kitchen. He told them of the owner's attempt to destroy the package and went on:

'I'd like to take Corram in.'

'Glory-hunting?' Simpson asked.

'They do say the Sheriff's Office likes to keep up its arrests' record,' Gotz went on.

'What's the caper?' Simpson continued, for both men knew more than glory-hunting or an attempt to improve the Sheriff's Office record of arrests lay behind the request.

'He might be able to help us with the Turn-Off killing,' Brad explained.

'Did he do it?' Simpson inquired.

'I don't reckon so. But he might help us get the guy who did, handled right.'

'You mean he might get all helpful and willing if he thought he saw a way out of this tight?' Gotz asked.

'Could be,' Brad said. 'It's worth a try, if you'll help me to set him up.'

'Bring him in,' Simpson offered. 'I saw a photograph of the victim. Whoever did it wants nailing bad.'

On his return, Brad found a remarkable change had come over the two men. Even knowing what lay ahead, he felt surprised at what he saw. Simpson's face held a coldly savage expression. No oil-painting at any time – his broken nose and scar dated from college football injuries rather than a brawl with a desperate criminal – Gotz looked brutal and eager to start working Corram over.

'This the bastard?' Simpson rasped.

'Sure,' Brad replied, watching the apprehension creep over Corram's face.

'Tried to destroy the evidence, huh?' Gotz said, taking a wicked leather-covered billie from his jacket pocket and slapping it against his palm idly. 'I don't like that one lil bit.'

'We'll tend to him,' Simpson promised, cracking his right knuckles in his left palm.

'Hey, hold it!' Brad put in as all the colour left Corram's face. 'You guys aren't—'

'Naw!' Simpson sneered. 'We aren't— Not much, anyways.'

'I'm not standing for any rough stuff!' Brad snapped.

'Just how the hell does it become any of your business?' Gotz growled. 'We only want to talk to the guy.'

'From the expression on Gotz's face, talk was the last thing he planned to do. Certainly Corram, watching the scarred features, did not doubt what his fate would be when left alone with the two detectives. Although clean in Gusher City – because he had not been caught at anything rather than by virtue of living a blameless life – Corram had had considerable experience with peace officers. He knew that some of them did work prisoners over; although far less than liberal-intellectuals preferred to imagine. Figuring he had come across two fuzz who enjoyed beating folk up, he felt scared at the thought of what would happen when Brad left the room.

'Sure we do,' Simpson agreed, grinding his right fist into the left palm. 'There's nothing we like better than talking to some crud who tries to destroy evidence on us.'

'I'm not standing for—!' Brad started.

'Nobody's asking you to!' Simpson barked. 'Get back to the Sheriff's Office and leave us do our work.'

'I'm taking him with me!' Brad stated.

'The hell you are!' Simpson barked. 'You're only a deputy and that don't rate higher than a detective.'

'And we've been detectives longer than you've been a deputy,' Gotz went on.

'So you want to play at pulling rank, huh!' Brad barked and went to the door. 'Can you come in here, Sergeant Fayde?'

Having already sent Hale to the D.P.S. Building in the second r.p. car to arrive, Alice had nothing to delay her appearance.

'What is it?' she asked.

'*Detective* Simpson objects to us taking Mr. Corram in,' Brad told her.

Although Brad had not discussed his intentions with her, Alice caught on immediately. Knowing Simpson to be a sergeant, taken with the men's expressions, told her everything.

'Come into the passage, Detective Simpson!' she snapped. 'Put the billy away, Detective Gotz.'

Muttering sullenly, Gotz obeyed. Then he stood and scowled in his most malevolent manner at Corram. Waiting until the door had closed on the other three peace officers, Gotz spat at Corram's feet.

'Just wait until we get you alone, buddy-buddy,' the detective hissed.

Once in the passage, Simpson's face reverted to being pleasant and amiable.

'I can't get my kids to do a thing I tell them,' he said.

'You don't look at them right,' Brad told him. 'Damned if you didn't near on convince me.'

'You should see him play the balcony scene from "Romeo and Juliet" with Harry,' Alice said. 'What's it all about, Brad?'

'Look, Vern,' Brad answered. 'You'd have one helluva chore proving anything on Corram.'

'So?' Simpson asked.

'Let Alice and me have him. If he co-operates, we fix it that the charges you're going to bring are dropped.'

'And leave him free to do the same thing again?' the Narcotics Detail man snapped.

'Not in this town,' Alice stated. 'We'll fix it so that he'll be

134

only too willing to leave. That won't be hard to do.'

'I can't go as far as saying I'll drop the charges,' Simpson warned.

'We know that,' Alice replied. 'And we'll leave the bosses settle it at the Office. How about it, Vern?'

'We've got the "h", that's the big thing,' Simpson replied quietly. 'Seems Tippy shook his tail this morning. Likely he didn't want to leave the package lying around for too long.'

'Or figured you'd not expect him to make his move so soon,' Brad guessed. 'I reckon Corram's near on set up now. A lil bit more prodding and he's ours, Alice.'

'Sure,' she replied. 'Let's go back in.'

'Hey!' Brad said to Simpson as they turned towards the door. 'Which of you plays Juliet?'

'Harry,' the detective grinned. 'Only there's times I don't see him in the part.'

Corram almost jumped into the air when the door jerked open and Simpson stamped in. While the deputies and detective had been outside, Corram had spent his time watched by Gotz's unwinking eyes. The brief period they had been gone seemed far longer to the now thoroughly-scared man.

'So take it up with the Chief of Detectives!' Alice was saying as she followed Simpson. 'I've heard about how you pair handle prisoners.'

'Yeah—!' Simpson began.

'Brad, go with them and see they bring him to the Sheriff's Office without side-trips to the little room downstairs,' Alice ordered.

'Yo!' Brad replied.

'Do we have to take this guff, Vern?' Gotz growled.

'Only 'til we get to Headquarters,' Simpson answered. 'We can wait. I dearly love waiting.'

Alice left the room. Collecting Brad's M.G., she drove to the D.P.S. Building. Asking to see the sheriff, she explained to Jack Tragg and McCall what Brad hoped to achieve. As she expected, her superiors gave their approval and assistance.

Back at the store, Brad and the detectives kept Corram waiting with growing anxiety to allow Alice time to make the arrangements. Then they let him collect his jacket, left a patrolman to watch his property, and took the storekeeper across town. Gotz carried the package, addressed to 'J. Burton, 18 Rio Grande Street, Gusher City', and hoped there would be some way they could prove Tippy Hale came to collect it.*

The drive to the D.P.S. Building did nothing to lessen Corram's fear. All the time he kept remembering that he might soon be left at the tender mercies of the two detectives. Nor did his arrival at the building make him feel better. Taken into McCall's office, he was subjected to a scowling scrutiny by the sheriff, first deputy and the captain commanding the Narcotics Detail.

'This's him, huh?' Jack Tragg growled. 'Damned if I see what all the fuss's over.'

'Or me,' McCall went on.

'Way I see it,' Captain Baines continued, 'this crud tried to destroy evidence that my men needed. I say they should have him.'

'Heave him into an interrogation room, Counter,' McCall ordered. 'Then come back here. You've got some questions to answer.'

Deputy Tupman followed Brad into the interrogation room and leaned against the wall, eyeing Corram coldly.

'So you caused a coloured gentleman grief, huh?' the Negro deputy said menacingly after Brad left. 'I can't say I like that one lil bit.'

After that Tupman lapsed into silence. Already set into motion, Corram's imagination did the rest. The storekeeper knew – although no liberal-intellectual would want to believe it – that some Negro officers would work over a white prisoner out of racial hatred. From Tupman's expression, he was one of them.

---

* In that luck favoured the detectives. On examination, Latent Prints found both Hale's and Rimmer's fingerprints on the box inside the wrappings. Trying to save himself, Rimmer talked. When they had received the heroin, the two men wanted to dispose of it between Friday and Monday when they would pass it on. So they made up a package, placed the correct value of postage stamps on it and addressed it to Corram's store. Carrying a duplicate package in plain sight, in case he was followed, Rimmer had dropped the genuine article into a mail-box without being detected.

So, one way and another, Corram was in a state where he welcomed the sight of Brad's face after so many hostile sets of features. That was what the peace officers had been building up to from the start. Simpson and Gotz were sergeants, equivalent in rank to the deputies. Relying on Corram not knowing that, they had played the rank-pulling game and brought it off. The attitudes of the other men had gone further to render Corram susceptible to Brad's 'sympathy'.

'Narcotics want you bad, Al,' Brad remarked after Tupman left them alone, offering the man a cigarette. 'Simpson and Gotz're fixing to nail your hide to the wall, way they're talking.'

'Why me?' Corram wailed. 'How do I know what these guys have in their mail?'

'You were trying to destroy that parcel when I came in,' Brad reminded him.

'I was trying to destroy all the mail,' Corram protested. 'That's one of the understandings I give; that I destroy all the mail if it looks like falling into the wrong hands.'

'I believe you, Al— But can you prove it?'

Clearly Corram could not. All agreements about his services were strictly verbal. Anybody who used an accommodation address had good, and private, reasons for doing so. So Corram doubted if any of his clients would even admit they had mail sent to him.

'I – I just happened to grab up that parcel first—' Corram faltered, then he remembered his earlier thoughts on how Brad came to dress so well. 'You saw I'd got some letters in my hand as well as the parcel.'

'Did I?'

'I can go up t—' Corram began.

'Al!' Brad interrupted gently. 'My pappy gives me ten grand a year allowance above my salary from the Sheriff's Office. What would I need your penny-ante bribe for?' He paused to let the words sink in, then went on, 'I don't want money, I want information.'

'I don't rat on the mob behind Tippy Hale!' Corram yelped.

'I don't expect you to,' Brad replied. 'All I want to know is about a guy called James M. Pallfret.'

'Who?'

'So play it that way,' Brad snorted and turned towards the door.

At which point Corram remembered that the big blond was probably his only friend in the building.

'Look, deputy,' he said in a conciliatory tone. 'I got a heap of names on my books. I don't dig this Pallfret.'

'You're wasting my time then,' Brad growled. 'I'll let Simpson and Gotz—'

'Hold it!' Corram squawked, producing a notebook from his jacket's breast pocket. 'Lemme see what I've got on him.' He turned the pages, stopping at one and began to read, 'James M. Pallfret. Parcel from Turner & Grail Sports House, New York City. Weighed just over two and a half pounds, was about eighteen inches square and four inches deep. Arriv—'

'All right, you've convinced me,' Brad said, turning and sitting down. 'Now, what did the guy look like?'

'He only come in twice—'

'You're stalling again.'

'What do I get out of this?'

'A whole hide and a chance to leave Gusher City without going to jail,' Brad replied. 'Or maybe you'd like to take things up with Simpson and Gotz?'

'Naw!' Corram stated emphatically. 'Pallfret's a tallish guy, maybe five-eleven, skinny. He had long hair and a beard, but he was cleaner and better dressed than most hippies. Tell you one thing, he works for the *Mirror*.'

'How do you know?' Brad asked.

'I tailed him after he collected the parcel. Saw him leave his car in the *Mirror*'s parking lot, then he went into their building like he belonged there.'

'How close were you to him?'

'Close enough to know it was him even though he'd took off his beard and long hair.'

'Would you recognize him?'

'I dunno. I wasn't all that close. So help me, I'm levelling with you.'

'Know something?' Brad said quietly. 'I think you are.'

'You'll help me then?' Corram asked eagerly.

'Let's go see the sheriff,' Brad replied.

CHAPTER NINETEEN

ALTHOUGH Jack Tragg and his deputies had not expected such a windfall to come out of Brad's scheme, they wasted no time in preparing to exploit it to the full.

By the time Brad had persuaded Corram to co-operate, various aspects of the affair had been settled. Already the District Attorney had told the sheriff that he doubted if they could make a charge of complicity stick against Corram. Any reasonably competent lawyer would be able to 'prove' that the storekeeper knew nothing of the package's contents and had merely tried to follow a verbal agreement with *all* his clients by destroying their mail if'it seemed likely to fall into the wrong hands. The lawyer would then claim that it had been no more than chance that Corram picked up the package first.

So Jack Tragg decided that they would lose nothing by letting Corram believe he could avoid being charged if he helped them nail the killer of Fairy Manders. Satisfied with the arrest of Tippy Hale and Rimmer, the head of the Narcotics Detail raised no objections. Even if Corram chose to remain in Gusher City, the publicity attending the nar-cotics case would ruin his postal accommodation business. Probably he would leave town as soon as possible to avoid facing Hale's employers and, anyway, his usefulness to them had ended.

'Which brings us to how we use Corram,' Jack told Alice, Brad and McCall as they gathered in his office.

'Do we need him?' Alice asked. 'Tony's taken a composite sketch of Vassel with a beard to the Starlight Grill to ask if the waiter recognizes him, and Lars went to see the clerk who hired him the car with another. On top of that, I.C.R.'ve come through to say the fingerprints on the Ford's hand-brake are his.'

Working with their usual speed and efficiency, I.C.R. at Austin had not only matched the fingerprints, but sent details of why they had a copy on file. Vassel had been arrested in Austin, taking part in a riot following a 'Kennedy Is A War-Monger' demonstration he helped organize at the time of the Cuban confrontation and again for helping to wreck a sporting-goods store in San Antonio during an anti-firearms protest march following the assassination of President Kennedy. As he had kept out of trouble around Gusher City, his fingerprints were not on the local files.

'That ties him in on the try at you,' Jack admitted. 'But it doesn't prove he killed Fairy Manders. He'd say it was an accident on the Turn-Off and he was too scared of police brutality to stop when he realized it was you he'd nearly run off the road.'

'He was following us,' Brad protested. 'And before anybody asks me, no, I can't prove it.'

'So you pick him up and he claims he was just tailing you as a reporter looking for a story,' Jack warned. 'There's no evidence to prove he wasn't.'

'He's been calling here and asking about the case ever since the news broke,' McCall went on. 'So he'd reckon he had to tail you because we refused to hand out information.'

'How about if either the waiter or the clerk identifies him from the sketches?' Alice wanted to know, although she could guess at the answer.

'That'd not be proof we could put before the jury, his lawyer would tear it to shreds,' Jack replied. 'We need something stronger before we take him before a judge. Now if we'd a witness—'

'Which we don't have,' McCall pointed out.

'Maybe we do,' Alice put in quietly.

'How do you mean, Alice?' Jack inquired, studying the girl's face.

Instead of answering the sheriff's question, Alice looked at her partner. 'Just how willing is Corram to co-operate, Brad?'

'Way we got his nerves jumping, I'd say the whole hawg down to the teensiest bristle at the end of its tail,' Brad replied.

'What's the game, Alice?' Jack demanded.

'I reckon we should let Vassel think there was a witness to the killing,' she answered. 'If Corram will help, we could do it.'

Quickly Alice explained her scheme. The men listened attentively and two pairs of male eyes turned to the sheriff. For a short time Jack Tragg did not comment, then he nodded.

'It could work. There's an added inducement for Corram. Tom Baxter called me this morning. He wants to post a five grand reward for anybody who can give evidence that helps us nail Fairy Manders' killer.'

'Aye, that'll interest Corram,' McCall agreed. 'But doing it could be dangerous for him. Leave us not forget that Vassel has killed once. Likely he doesn't have the gun—'

'I think he does,' Brad interjected. 'He had it up to last Monday and S.I.B. combed the woods without finding it. I figure that if he didn't throw it away straight after killing with it, he'll still have it.'

'Then get a warrant and go search his pad for it,' McCall suggested.

'He'll have it hidden, but not in his apartment,' Brad objected. 'If we make a search, he'll know we're on to him.'

'Why will he still have the gun, Brad?' Jack asked.

'It's only a hunch,' Brad reminded. 'But I reckon he's such an egotistic bastard that he'll reckon there's no way us incompetent Fascist-hyena badges can tie him to Fairy Manders.'

'I'll go with Brad on that,' Alice stated. 'To Vassel, keeping the gun would be a sign of his brilliance and superiority over us. Look at how he's been acting since news of the killing came out. He was up here asking about it on Thursday afternoon and has been calling in since. Then he tailed me across town, followed us out to the Baxter place and tried to kill us on the way back.'

'He didn't use a gun for it,' McCall pointed out.

'He'd be too smart for that,' Alice replied. 'Probably he didn't have it along with him. Anyways, making it look like an accident was better. It would delay the investigation and give him a better chance of getting away with killing her. We were getting too close to him. Whoever took over would have to start almost from scratch. The longer it took to reach witnesses, the less chance of them remembering anything.'

'So we get Corram to do his part,' Jack said. 'What'll Vassel's reaction be when he learns there's a witness?'

'He'll run,' McCall guessed.

'Maybe not,' Alice answered. 'He's got a good job here, one he'd not get the equal of without plenty of work and effort. No, he'll either agree to pay Corram off—'

'Or try to kill him,' Brad finished. 'We'll have to fix it so that the try is made with the gun.'

'I still reckon he'll run,' McCall objected.

'Not if he reckons we've still no idea that he's connected with Fairy Manders,' Alice disagreed. 'And I think we can fix it so he believes we're going off in the wrong direction.'

'How?' Jack asked.

'With the help of P.R.,' Alice replied. 'And Helen Whitsall.'

At five o'clock, his day's work finished, Tony Vassel left the *Mirror*'s offices. Walking along Crown Street with a self-satisfied smirk playing on his face, he entered the parking lot where he had left his car. A small delivery truck with, 'MERCURY FLOWER PARLOUR' on its sides stood to the right of the reporters' Ford Mustang but he hardly glanced at it. Instead Vassel's full attention was on the man who leaned against the Mustang – and who looked disturbingly familiar.

'Hey there!' the man greeted, making no attempt to move although he was standing in front of the driver's door. 'Thought you'd be along about now.'

While Vassel openly professed his admiration and companionship for the down-trodden working-class people of the world, he had no desire to associate with them after office hours. He also expected such of them as he met to show gratitude for his support of their cause by acting with deference and respect in his presence. So he resented the man's attitude of easy familiarity.

'What can I do for you?' Vassel asked brusquely.

'Where do we talk?' the man demanded, in a voice which expressed anything but deference and respect.

'If you've a story—' Vassel began, then remembered where he had last seen the man.

'I've a story. It's a gas.'

'Come and see me tomorrow—'

'Now!' the man corrected.

'I've no ti—' Vassel began.

'You – or the cops, Mr. James M. Pallfret.'

Vassel sucked in a deep breath. Hearing his assumed name mentioned, he felt his uneasiness increase. There was a glint in Corram's eyes that the reporter did not like; a hint of common knowledge, or a guilty secret shared.

'Pallfret?' Vassel said, trying desperately to sound unconcerned. 'My name—'

'I know what your name is,' Corram interrupted. 'And that you had a package come to me from Turner & Grail in New York with James M. Pallfret on it.'

'I – I don't know what you mean,' 'Vassel breathed, glancing around him nervously.

Nobody was close enough to hear the conversation, for which Vassel felt very grateful. A patrolman was strolling in a leisurely manner along the other side of Crown Street and the reporter looked at him. So did Corram, giving a low chuckle and saying, 'Maybe the cop over there'd know what I mean. All you have to do is call him over and ask.'

Which was the last thing that Vassel intended to do. Nor did his liberal-intellectual aversion to peace officers, as tools of the capitalist society, cause his desire to keep the patrolman ignorant of his affairs. Up until meeting Corram, Vassel had felt satisfied that he was safe from detection as the killer of Fairy Manders.

Sure the deputies had identified the body far quicker than he expected; but he had felt sure there was nothing to connect him with it. On every meeting with the girl, he had worn his wig and false beard. How well they worked as a disguise showed in that he had walked by friends and acquaintances wearing them and not been recognized.

Even learning Fairy Manders' identity seemed to lead the deputies farther away from the truth. According to a newcast on the local radio network, and a P.R. hand-out to the press, the investigating officers had finally discovered that the victim was Fairy Manders, a top-ranking girl wrestler. Showing the incompetence one could expect from a millionaire's son Deputy Sheriff Bradford Counter was now chasing false leads among the girl's opponents and had brought in another wrestler, Helen Whitsall, for questioning. By the time the deputies finished checking out all the other debased crud to do with girl wrestling, there would be no chance of anybody remembering the bearded man who met Fairy Manders around town.

So Vassel had left the *Mirror* building with a feeling of contentment and delight at having completely baffled the inefficient Fascist peace officers, believing himself safe— And then he met Corram.

'What do you want?' Vassel hissed.

'Now that depends on you,' Corram answered. 'I don't reckon the law'd be interested in hearing about you eating steak, French-fried onions, and boiled potatoes followed by apple-turn-over in the Starlight Grill last Monday. Except that you were eating it at a table with Fairy Manders.'

Stark, raw fear twisted at Vassel's face. Always he had imagined himself as a kind of super-intelligent, ultra-tough intellectual reporter portrayed in the *Saints And Sinners* or *The Name of the Game* television shows; capable of outwitting dumb, ignorant cops and outsmarting cheap grifters with ease. Given his chance to do the latter, his courage oozed away and his superior intelligence refused to function. All he did was to stand and stare at the man in horror.

'Y – You saw me—' he began.

'I like to keep tabs on the marks who use my address,' Corram explained when the words trailed off. 'Especially any who use assumed names to buy guns from out-of-town stores. So I tailed you around, learned who you are. Saw you in the Starlight Grill last Monday and hadn't anything better to do, so I took out after you. I was thinking, when you went up the Turn-Off—'

'Get in here, quick!' Vassel snarled, indicating the car. Some more of the *Mirror* employees were approaching the parking lot and he did not wish them to see him with Corram.

'Nix, sonny,' the storekeeper replied. 'My mammy didn't raise any half-witted kids. We meet tonight and we meet alone.'

'W – Where?'

'You know the lake in Evans Park?'

'I know it.'

'Go to the public boating house, where you can hire boats in the daytime,' Corram instructed. 'Be there at nine-fifteen. Walk along the path in front of the cabin, the one with the flowering dogwood tree at its right side. Turn down the second path and to the left and I'll be waiting for you.'

'A – And if I don't come?' Vassel breathed.

'At nine-thirty I take what I have to the cops,' Corram answered calmly. 'Its your choice.'

'I'll be there!' the reporter promised and climbed into the car as Corram moved away from the door.

Fighting down a desire to turn his car and try to run Corram down, Vassel drove out of the parking lot. In his anxiety, he failed to notice a green Dodge sedan driven by a Negro pull out and follow him.

Despite his victim having gone, Corram made no attempt to leave the lot. Instead he leaned against the side of the delivery truck and watched the other *Mirror* employees collect their cars and go. Then he walked to the rear of the truck and its doors opened. Alice Fayde climbed out, followed by Brad Counter.

The truck was one of the Department of Public Safety's disguised stake-out vehicles. Although it appeared to belong to a store or business in the city – the name on the sides being interchangeable – it served to allow peace officers to hide and keep a suspected person or building under surveillance. Sitting in the body of the truck, the deputies watched and listened to the meeting with Vassel.

'How was I?' Corram inquired grinning ingratiatingly.

'Either you're a damned good actor, or you've had practice at putting the bite on people,' Alice answered. 'You never gave him anything he could definitely claim to be a blackmail attempt.'

While not sure whether to accept Alice's comment as complimentary, Corram decided against antagonizing her. He still believed that he had had a narrow escape from a brutal beating, followed by an appearance before a judge and receiving a jail sentence. So he wanted nothing to go wrong with his chances of gaining freedom.

'Reckon he's your man?' he asked.

'Don't you?' Alice countered.

'Yeah,' Corram decided. 'He'd've called that harness bull over if he'd been clean. The place I picked's just what you wanted. Thick bushes on both sides of the path, so nobody can see what's doing. Nine-fifteen's the best time. It's too late for kids, the boating lake's closed, and too early for the moon-and-June set.'

It had been decided that Corram would suggest a meeting place to conclude the 'blackmail' attempt if Vassel did not say enough to incriminate himself in the parking lot. As he had not, Corram went ahead with the plan.

'He'll either show or run,' Brad Counter remarked.

'Dick Tupman's on his tail if he runs,' Alice replied. 'let's get back to the office. Helen wants to be finished in time for her bout tonight.'

On hearing Alice's suggestion, Helen Whitsall had willingly agreed to co-operate if doing so helped to capture Fairy Manders' killer. So she had been brought to the Sheriff's Office, ostensibly to be questioned about the murder but really to help keep Vassel's confidence in his safety. Helen's only stipulation had been that they tried to get through with her in time for the bout she was billed to appear in at the Evans Hill Armoury.

'Reckon we'll have time to go and see her fight before setting up in the Park, boss-lady?' Brad inquired, after shutting Corram in the rear of the truck. 'Waste's a sin and it'd be plumb sinful to waste those tickets she gave us.'

'That's what I thought,' Alice replied. 'So I fixed it that they won't be wasted. I gave them to Mick Rafferty and Tommy Chu.'

Brad favoured his partner with an exasperated glare. 'Maybe Great-Grandpappy Mark'd have known what to do with you,' he said. 'But I'm damned if I do.'

'And that's just the way I like it,' Alice assured him. 'Let's go and get ready for tonight.'

CHAPTER TWENTY

VASSEL had been almost sick with anxiety since the meeting with Corram. On reaching his apartment, he locked himself in and started to pack his belongings. Even as he debated whether to cross the Juarez Bridge into Mexico, or to take his car and head for New York, he saw the futility of flight. If he failed to keep the appointment, Corram would inform the Sheriff's Office of his connection with the dead girl.

Much as Vassel liked to pretend that the local law was in the hands of incompetent bunglers, who became peace officers because they were too stupid or idle to perform constructive work, he knew the pretence to be false. He could not forget how quickly Alice Fayde and Brad Counter had learned Fairy Manders' identity and located her employers. While they might be checking on other girl wrestlers as possible suspects, they would look into any other lead. In fact he felt that they would be even more diligent if they saw a chance of getting something on him.

Once Corram told his story, the deputies would check it out with that deliberate, painstaking patience which, rather than blindingly brilliant, split-second deduction, solved crimes. By visiting the Starlight Grill, they might find others who had seen Vassel with Fairy Manders. In fact somebody might remember seeing them come to his apartment that fatal Monday evening. S.I.B.'s handwriting experts could prove that Vassel had filled out the order blank to Turner and Grail and obtained the gun. Maybe Cornelius, the firearms expert, could say from the bullets what type of revolver had killed the girl.

Flight was still not the answer.

Not only would Corram direct the law to him, but he would be forced to start his career almost from scratch if

147

he ran. He had a lucrative position with the *Gusher City Mirror* which he did not care to abandon. On top of that, he had sold a story to a television production company and hoped to continue working for that medium. He could not do so if he was on the run from the law.

The programme he had written was on the local network that night. Turning on his set, he sought to drive his problems away by watching. He had not informed any of his colleagues about his first effort being televised. Like the Russians on their space programme, he wanted to be sure of success before announcing the attempt had been made.

Watching the programme, he could barely concentrate. The action was one of his pet day-dreams and its hero identified with himself. Yet he could not sit back and enjoy the hero's triumph, or the fact that he put over a 'message'. He was caught up in a real life drama and wanted to get out of it.

Switching off the set, he sank into a chair. He wondered if he might arrange for one of his underworld contacts to meet Corram and close the storekeeper's mouth. The idea seemed little better than flight, he decided. While he might try to glorify them as victims of the capitalist society's bigotry, none of the criminals he knew struck him as suitable. He could offer no satisfactory reason for wanting Corran killed. Nor would he be better off if he arranged a contract on Corram without explaining his motives. Doing so would only remove the storekeeper and leave Vassel in the hands of another cheap grifter.

That he might call on his companions at the *Mirror* for help never entered his head. They were all of liberal persuasions like him, mean-minded and with all the vices of their kind. He knew there had been much resentment when he attained the highly-desired role of film, television, theatre and literary critic for the paper – as it entailed extra pay for less work. So those below him would use anything he told them to remove him and make way for themselves, while those above would never jeopardize their careers by offering to help.

Vassel's parents, to whom he always referred as being a pair of drunken, social-climbing, middle-class slobs, lived in the East. Since starting to earn enough money to live without their financial support, he had lost touch with them. So Vassel was alone.

By eight o'clock Vassel had reached his decision. Corram's mouth must be closed; and in such a way that it could not be brought home to the reporter.

Changing into his psychedelic shirt, which he had not worn since the abortive attempt at killing the deputies, he made his plans. He collected the revolver from its hiding-place in the cellar, checking that its cylinder carried six British bullets. Then he tucked it into his waistband, put the wig and false beard into his jacket pockets and was ready to leave. He had the problem licked. Kill Corram and let the law hunt for a hippie. If anybody saw Vassel the hair and beard would give the desired false impression.

Leaving the apartment building at nine o'clock, Vassel entered his Mustang. The night was dark and if he noticed the Dodge sedan parked across the street, he attached no importance to it. Although the sedan had been parked in the same place for over three and a half hours, neither the patrolmen walking their beat nor the prowling r.p. cars paid any attention to it. An observant person might have noticed that the car's occupants had changed. At eight o'clock a pair of white men had arrived, conversed with the Negro who had followed Vassel home, then climbed into the car as he walked away.

Seated in the Dodge, Deputies Larsen and Valenca watched the reporter drive off in the Mustang. While Larsen started the engine and followed, Valenca took up a Voice Commander radio.

'UC 5 to Cen-Con,' Valenca said.

'Cen-Con by,' came back the answer.

'Suspect on move in easterly direction. On his tail. "Code One"?'

'Roger, UC 5. Will inform reception committee. Over.'

Alice and Brad had spent the evening in and around the D.P.S. Building. Reports from the stake-out on Vassel reached them from time to time. While unable to watch the actual apartment, Larsen and Valenca stayed out front and arranged for a detective from the local House to cover the building's rear entrance. During the afternoon the smashed panel had been replaced and Corram's store closed. Deputy Ortega staked the store out after Corram's meeting with Vassel, in case the reporter tried to reach its owner ahead of schedule.

While eating a meal at the Badge Diner, Alice and Brad watched Vassel's television show. In it a liberal-intellectual reporter spent most of his time boasting how he abhorred violence, then escaped from the clutches of a neo-Fascist arms training group by licking three of them in a fight, grabbing a gun and routing some thirty more with very accurate shooting.

'Whooee!' Alice said as they left the diner, neither having been present when Vassel's name appeared on the screen credits. 'So that's the kind of man we're going up against.'

'If Vassel had a script-writer like the crud who thought that up, I'd be scared to go against him,' Brad replied. 'Did you notice how all the bad guys talked with Southern drawls?'

'Don't all the bad guys these days?' Alice asked. 'Anyways, I love you; even if you are from the South. So leave us not start reading social comment into the shows, huh.'

'You're the boss, ma'am,' Brad answered. 'Let's go to the Park. Maybe Vassel'll start saying "you-all" and "honey-chile" when we get him.'

With that sentiment, Brad took Alice's arm and they walked back to the D.P.S. Building. There they put aside all levity, made the final check on their arrangements and then gathered the people concerned to head for Evans Park.

The Enfield revolver gouged into Vassel's flesh as he climbed out of the Mustang. Leaving the car in an all but deserted parking lot, he crossed the street and entered the Park. He did not look back, or he would have seen the Dodge sedan halt and Valenca using the radio.

Approaching the boat-house by the lake, Vassel touched the beard he had donned before leaving the Mustang. Then he reached under his jacket to grip the comforting butt of the gun. Going along the path by the flowering dogwood tree, he watched for the second turning on the left. A feeling of elation filled him. Soon he would remove the only person who could definitely link him with Fairy Manders. A cheap crook, a parasite. In doing so Vassel would prove again his superior intelligence by baffling the peace officers.

Turning on to the second path he came to, Vassel found himself in a gloomy tunnel between thick bushes. He slid out the revolver, holding it behind his back. At the same moment he realized that he was gripping the butt in his bare hand. That was a mistake, but would not prove serious. After killing Corram, he would wipe the gun clean, take it to the Rio Grande and throw it into a deep pool from which it could not be recovered.

Passing around a corner, Vassel found a shape blocking his way. He barely held down a gasp of surprise.

'You're late, buddy-buddy,' Corram's voice said from the shape. 'I was just figuring on going to the cops.'

'How much do you want?' Vassel asked, walking forward.

'That's near enough!' Corram growled while some thirty feet still separated them. Far enough for the bullet-proof vest he wore to stop any revolver bullet.

The words brought the reporter to a halt. Peering through the darkness, he tried to see if the other held a gun. While he could see no sign of one, he felt it likely that the storekeeper would be armed.

'All right,' Vassel said. 'What's the bite?'

'For forgetting you bought the gun?' Corram asked. 'Or to forget I saw you kill Fairy Manders?'

'Both!' the reporter snarled. 'How much for both?'

'Why'd you kill her, Vassel?' Corram asked.

'Because she—!'

Starting to reply, Vassel chopped off his words. There should have been no need for Corram to ask that question if he had witnessed the killing. Perhaps he knew far less than he pretended! Maybe he had only guessed about the killing and made the rendezvous in the hope of learning more.

If so, he had heard enough and must die!

Bringing the gun from behind his back, Vassel tried to line it on the dark shape. A movement among the bushes at the left diverted the reporter's attention. Then lights glowed on either side of the track, illuminating the scene. Flashbulbs popped near the lights. The reporter knew the cameras must be aiming at him – and on the incriminating revolver in his hand. Before he could think of throwing the gun away, he saw a shape loom out of the bushes, moving to stand before Corram.

It was Brad Counter. A low crowned, wide brimmed black Stetson covered his blond hair. He wore a black suit, dark blue shirt and matching cravat. Although he did not hold a weapon, his left hand rose in a leisurely manner to unbutton and open his jacket.

'Drop the gun, Vassel,' Brad ordered. 'You're under arrest.'

Backing off a couple of steps, Vassel made no attempt to obey. Instead he kept the revolver lined in Brad's direction. Fury filled the reporter as he realized that he had been tricked into a confession that would hold up in court.

'Keep back Counter!' Vassel screeched. 'Keep away, or I'll shoot you!'

'Like you shot Fairy Manders?' Brad asked, starting to walk slowly forward.

'J – Just like I killed her!' Vassel replied.

'So shoot,' Brad drawled calmly, continuing his steady advance. 'Go to it. Pull the trigger. You hit her six times as she came up that slope and didn't stop her. I'm bigger and stronger than she was. There's only one way you can stop me, Vassel. By shooting me in the head – and you don't shoot good enough to do that.'

'I – I'll show you if I don't!' the reporter croaked, falling back another pace.

'Your gun's not pointing at my head,' Brad stated. 'You'll have to lift it and take aim. Only you won't have time to do it. As soon as you start to lift your gun, I'll draw on you – and I won't miss.'

In the bushes, Alice stood behind two of the 110-volt, battery-powered floodlights – borrowed from the S.I.B.'s mobile laboratory unit – which had been brought to illuminate the scene. At her feet lay the Voice Commander radio with which she had kept in touch with Central Control and learned of Vassel's progress. In her hand, she held her Colt Commander automatic but she did not offer to fire. Next to her, Sam Hellman held his camera in the left hand, his right gripping a Colt Python revolver. Across the track, a second cameraman also held a gun. With him stood the *Lightning* reporter who had covered Flaker's false confes-

152

sion and had been invited along, without knowing why, to witness the meeting. Sweat trickled down the reporter's face as he watched Brad Counter walk empty-handed towards the barrel of Vassel's revolver.

'I – I'll kill you, Counter!' Vassel threatened.

'Try it,' Brad offered him, taking another unhurried stride forward. 'You saw how I can handle a gun last Saturday. And my gun's a helluva sight more powerful than that relic in your hands. Before you can use it, I'll put a bullet right into your guts.'

Soft-spoken though they might be, the words ripped into Vassel and froze his thoughts of how easy killing the speaker appeared. And Vassel wanted to kill. Not only as a means of escape, but out of all his bigoted hatred for a man better looking, better equipped physically and wealthier than himself. Yet he could not make his finger pull at the trigger.

All too vividly Vassel remembered how Brad had handled the big automatic on the previous Saturday. He could almost see again how the blond deputy stood apparently unarmed, then spun around and started shooting, with a balloon in the centre of a man-shaped target bursting each time he squeezed the trigger. More than that, Vassel could visualize how the English policeman had stood alongside Brad, the revolver already pointing at the target. Even with that much of a start, the Englishman only barely managed to beat the tall peace officer's shot. When the man had had to raise his gun shoulder high, he stood no chance against Brad Counter's lightning fast reflexes.

Which brought back to Vassel the shocking thought of the risk he had taken when he had tried to run Brad's M.G. off the road. Watching Brad shoot on Saturday, Vassel had suddenly realized just how dangerous the attempt had been. That had been the cause of the worry Brad saw on the reporter's face in the basement range.

Although Vassel's intellectual-reporter had faced and bluffed down an armed man during the television show, he could not produce the same heroic disregard for danger. Instead all he could think of was that Brad Counter had killed at least five men in the line of duty. *Men!* Armed and dangerous criminals. Not an unsuspecting girl. So, much as Vassel wanted to shoot, he lacked the guts to try.

'Drop it, Vassel!' Brad commanded, measuring the distance separating them with his eyes.

'I'll ki—!' the reporter screamed, trying to control his shaking hand and drawing back on the Enfield's trigger so that the hammer rose slowly.

Gliding forward another step, Brad lashed his left hand out and across. He struck Vassel's right wrist, batting it aside. In almost the same movement Brad's right arm bent and swung upwards. Hard knuckles crashed under the reporter's jaw. Jerked on to his toes by the impact, Vassel pitched over backwards. The revolver slipped from his limp fingers and the hammer returned to its normal position without gaining sufficient momentum to fire the waiting cartridge.

'That was for Fairy Manders,' Brad said softly.

Dashing forward, Alice fought to regain control of her churned-up emotions. She succeeded before she reached her partner's side. None of the anxiety she had felt showed as she looked down at the spread-eagled form of the unconscious Vassel.

'He can't be our man, Brad,' she said, thinking back to their conversation earlier that evening in the Badge Diner.

'How do you mean?' Brad demanded. 'We've got all the evidence, including the gun he used to kill her.'

'Sure we have,' Alice agreed with a smile. 'But he never spoke with a Southern drawl once.'

CHAPTER TWENTY-ONE

THE time was eleven o'clock. Alice, Brad, McCall, Jack Tragg and a policewoman stenographer stood or sat in a half circle around Vassel as he slumped on a chair in the sheriff's office. No longer did Vassel show arrogance, or drip smug condescension on the peace officers. Since being brought in, he had been placed on a line up, with false beard and wig, among eight hippies and identified by the clerk who rented out the Ford and the waiter from the Starlight Grill.

'You can't prove I killed her!' he said sullenly.

'We'll try,' Alice assured him. 'We've got you on two counts of attempted murder for starters.'

'Two?'

'Running us off the road on the Turn-Off's one of them.'

'That was an accident! I'd have stopped, but when I saw it was your car I was scared of what you'd do to me with no witnesses around.'

'How about trying to kill Corram?' Alice inquired.

'He was a blackmailer,' Vassel answered.

'You can't shoot a man for that,' Alice pointed out, 'even if he was blackmailing you — and we never heard him mention it, either in the Park or at the Crown Street parking lot.'

'You know about that?' the reporter gasped.

'We heard every word,' Alice replied.

'You couldn't have! There was nobody close enough— That delivery truck—'

'It's out back, in the official parking lot,' Brad told him. 'We'll make you as the owner of the gun. Turner and Grail only sold one in this area and its serial numbers matched your piece. Mr. Corram can identify you as the man who collected the package it came in.'

'It looks like that cheap grifter did all your work for you,' Vassel snarled.

'All he knew, except about you collecting the gun, we gave him,' Alice stated calmly.

'Don't snow me!' Vassel spat, glaring at her. 'He even told me what I had to eat that Monday night and where I was.'

'Which we told him,' Alice replied. 'We learned you'd been to the Starlight Grill and S.I.B. gave us the rest from an analysis of the vomit you left by the body. We figured your conscience would make you think Corram knew more than he did.'

A knock on the door heralded the arrival of Lieutenant Cornelius. 'I've run a comparison check. The Enfield's the gun that killed Fairy Manders. So I sent it to the lab. It hadn't been cleaned, there's blood and flesh on the lanyard ring and base of the butt.'

'That's something more against you, Vassel,' Brad said.

Then Alice had an inspiration. She remembered something which had emerged repeatedly during the questioning of people who knew Fairy Manders. Looking at Vassel and recalling his attitudes towards various things, she asked a question.

'What happened, Vassel. Did she discover you were writing an exposé on the evils of women wrestling and objected to it?'

Shock twisted the reporter's face. Even without his nod of agreement, the peace officers would have known that Alice had called the play correctly.

'That's just what happened,' the reporter confirmed. 'I saw her in a Green Valley bar and recognized her. I'd been planning an exposé on women wrestlers and grabbed a chance of meeting one. It would help me prove my case that they were nothing but trained acrobats pandering to the depraved tastes of a moronic section of the public. I made her easy and she let slip about the Baxters over in Calverton. At first she wouldn't talk about them, but I got her to say she'd take me to meet them. I wanted to see what kind of money-hungry cretins would degrade women that way, but I didn't get a chance.'

'Somebody tipped her to who and what you are?' Brad prompted as the man's story came to a halt.

'Yeah,' Vassel agreed bitterly. 'It was me. She met me on

156

Sunday and made a date to come to my place Monday evening, but she stalled about taking me to the Baxters. Fair enough, I could go out there on my own. She said she'd come to my pad on Monday and let me photograph her in her new bikini. That's what it started out as. Nobody saw me take her up to my pad. But I had to go out and make a call to another dame. I forgot that I'd started my exposé and it was in the typewriter. When I came back I could feel the chill. But she asked why we didn't go see the Baxters right then. I didn't catch on until we were going along the Turn-Off and she asked me to stop. I did and she got out of the car, took off her coat and dress. All she had on was that bikini. Well, she went down that slope and said I should come down to photograph her. I should need asking twice.

I went down after her. At the bottom she started asking who the hell I thought I was, writing a pack of lies, trash and rubbish about girl wrestlers. I tell you, I was scared. She was a trained wrestler—'

'I thought they were just acrobats?' Brad interrupted.

'Look, I'm a writer. I have a duty to expo—' Vassel blustered.

'Drop it!' Jack Tragg ordered. 'What happened next?'

'I ran back up the slope. The revolver was in the glove compartment, I'd put it there meaning to throw it into a canyon, or into the Rio Grande sometime. I got it out and pointed it at her. Honest, I only meant to frighten her, but the gun has a hair-trigger—'

Once more Brad cut into Vassel's flow of talk. 'That model Enfield can only be fired double-action. There's no way you can give it a hair-trigger.'

'All right!' the reporter croaked. 'So I meant to shoot her! You should have heard what she called me. ME! A cheap bigot. A lousy college-boy punk who could do nothing himself and wanted to bring everybody down to his own stinking level. That's what she called me.'

While very close to the truth, nothing else Fairy Manders could have said would so rouse the reporter's rage. For a moment he sat in the chair, breathing in and out deeply.

'So I shot her,' he went on at last. 'Only she didn't fall. I kept on shooting as she came up the slope. The last shot, the gun was almost touching her. She grabbed me and pulled me with her as she tumbled back down the slope. At the bottom I started to hit her with the gun's barrel to make her let loose. I just hit and hit. Then I realized what I'd done. There as blood on my clothes, but none on the ground. I dragged her between the bushes and was going to leave her. She'd told me she was leaving for St. Louis the next morning, so it might be days before she was missed. Even then, it could be weeks, or months before anybody found her body. Only I decided to take no chances. I damaged her eyes and burned off her hair to make identifying her more difficult. I'd have taken that damned bikini, but I was sick and couldn't face up to doing it. Anyway, it was only a cheap leopard print, I've seen plenty of them around.'

'What did you do with her clothes?' Alice asked.

'Made a bundle of them and my own, and burned them all in the incinerator at the civic dump,' Vassel answered. 'How did you get on to me?'

'The bikini was real leopard skin, not a nylon imitation,' Alice replied. 'But the Enfield led us to you.'

'I bought it in an assumed name,' Vassel protested. 'It couldn't have.'

'Your anti-gun exposé gave you away,' Brad went on.

'It couldn't!' Vassel gasped. 'I knew Turner and Grail wouldn't sell if I used my own name, so I put James M. Pallfret on the order blank. And I didn't mention the kind of gun I'd bought.'

'You didn't need,' Brad told him. 'Only a war surplus Enfield comes that cheap with eighteen British bullets and an instruction book.'

'Then that's how you knew!' Vassel breathed. He lifted his head and looked at the cold-eyed circle of peace officers around him. 'It was self-defence.'

'Let's hope the judge and jury feel the same way,' Jack Tragg growled.

Half an hour later Vassel signed a full confession which, eventually, took him to the death-house in the Walls, the main state prison at Huntsville.

Coming down in the elevator from delivering the reporter to the cell block, Brad found Alice waiting at the door. Before she could enter, Alvarez appeared from the watch commander's office.

'Alice, Brad,' he said. 'I'm sorry as hell to drop this on you, but there's been a hit-and-run kill on Beaumont Street and I don't have a team in the Office. Can you take it for me?'

While the first deputy said 'can you', it still counted as an order. Alice and Brad exchanged resigned looks and nodded their agreement. The Turn-Off case had been wrapped up, the killer of Fairy Manders – the girl everybody but one man loved – was under arrest and only the final accumulation of evidence to be presented at his trial remained to be completed. That could not be done until the following day. Until then life, and the work of enforcing the law, must go on.

'Let's go, Brad,' Alice said. 'Lordy lord. Who'd be a peace officer?'

Read more about the team of Alice Fayde and Bradford Counter in *The Point of Contact*, the next Rockabye County story.